MISSING PIECES

Missing Pieces

SANDY ASHER

 DELACORTE PRESS/NEW YORK

Published by
Delacorte Press
1 Dag Hammarskjold Plaza
New York, N.Y. 10017

Manufactured in the United States of America

Library of Congress Cataloging in Publication Data

Asher, Sandy
  Missing pieces.

  Summary: Heather's sophomore year brings many changes, but it is the tragic death of her father that enables her to change her relationship with her mother.
  [1. High schools—Fiction. 2. Schools—Fiction. 3. Mothers and daughters—Fiction. 4. Death—Fiction.]
  I. Title.
PZ7.A816Mi   1984   [Fic]
ISBN 0-385-29318-6
Library of Congress Catalog Card Number: 83-14381

For Harvey, Claire, Bebe, and George,
who are all in this with me

1

Thanksgiving, 1981, was different, all right. Mom cried in the cranberry sauce, and Mom is not an easy crier.

She seemed fine until then. She fussed at the turkey until Daddy finally whipped it away and started it smoking on the grill out back. She baked rolls and pies and prepared stuffing, and grudgingly turned loose the salad things so I could slice and chop and tear and toss. Somehow she got the table set, the pots and pans scrubbed, and the centerpiece arranged all at once. Thinking back on it now, I wonder if her superefficiency, even more amazing than usual, wasn't a clue that all was not well. If it was, I missed it.

Morning slipped quickly into afternoon, the temperature outside dropped, our kitchen windows steamed over, and Daddy donned hat, scarf, and gloves for rushed visits to his turkey.

"Heather! Jeannie! Stop what you're doing!" he suddenly shouted from the back door. Surprised, Mom dropped a handful of rolls outside the breadbasket. I was caught in the swinging door between the kitchen and the dining room, a forbidden spoonful of stuffing en route to my mouth.

"Behold the bird!" Daddy cried, and brought forth the turkey, smoked to a deep golden brown, its aroma filling the room with a tantalizing outdoorsy bitter-sweetness.

"It's a beauty," Mom told him.

"The best ever," I agreed.

"Thank you, ladies," Daddy said, marching his masterpiece to the counter. "Love that grill."

Mom and I exchanged a smile. We'd given Daddy the grill for his fiftieth birthday in September of last year. Before then, he'd never even boiled water; since then, he'd been grilling everything that couldn't jump the backyard fence and run for cover.

We soon had all the food arranged on the dining room table and sat smiling at each other across candles and chrysanthemums in autumn shades of bronze and gold.

"Everything's just perfect," Daddy said.

Mom had just lifted the bowl of cranberry sauce, and that's when she began to cry.

"Jean, what is it?" Daddy asked.

"Nothing. Not a thing. I'm fine," Mom said, pressing a napkin to her mouth with her free hand and blinking her eyes furiously to fight back the tears. Daddy gently took the bowl out of her hand and set it down. Then Mom drew in one long trembling breath and brought herself back under control.

"I'm okay," she said. "Just tired, I guess. Hot-stove syndrome. Let's eat."

So we ate. Daddy told a couple of silly jokes he'd heard at the office, and Mom and I groaned in response, then laughed anyway. No one mentioned Uncle Will,

Daddy's older brother, a widower who'd lived with us for six years until his second stroke forced him into a nursing home last winter. And no one mentioned my brother, Eddie, who'd graduated from college in June and immediately left for Oregon with his new wife, Marie, to live near her parents and "learn the ropes" at their department store. Thanksgiving had always meant the four of us plus, for a long while, Uncle Will, plus, as of last year, Marie. This Thanksgiving was different, all right, and as if an unspoken rule prevailed, no one mentioned it.

"Amazing how little time it takes to eat a meal, after all the hours it takes to prepare it," Daddy commented when we were all dutifully stuffed until we could stuff no more.

"And how long it takes to clean up afterward," I added, gathering his dish and mine as Mom loaded herself down with more plates, bowls, trays, and glasses than it seemed possible for one person to handle— especially one so short she has to sit on a pillow to drive. Through the swinging door we paraded, Daddy bringing up the rear with the remains of his turkey. Somehow the kitchen seemed less lonely than the dining room, maybe because we could fill the empty spaces better with busywork.

When we finally shuffled out of the kitchen and into the living room, I fell limp into an easy chair and Mom curled up in her favorite corner of the sofa, kicked off her shoes, and let her dark head come to rest on one plump little arm. Daddy stopped at the stereo and put on a recording of his favorite opera, *Rigoletto*. With what felt like my last ounce of energy, I managed to smile as he settled back in his corner of the sofa, eyes shut, listening so intently he was practically soaking the music up through his pores like vitamin D from the sun. I glanced sideways at Mom and caught the flicker of a smile. We both knew what was coming: Daddy's favorite aria.

When it hit, Daddy rose to his feet as usual to bellow along in off-key rapture. A few bars into it he pulled Mom up and whirled her around, warbling so horribly, so hilariously, she and I couldn't help but burst out laughing. The picture was every bit as bizarre as the sound: a waltzing Jack Sprat and his barefoot little wife struggling to keep up on tiptoe.

"What?" Daddy demanded in mock outrage, clasping a hand to his bald spot and helping Mom make her dizzy way back to her seat. "What's so funny? What's the joke?"

The more he protested, the harder we laughed, all to a deafening crescendo of music. Waving us aside impatiently, Daddy dove in for the final bars, hands clasped beneath his chin, eyes heavenward, voice soaring against the pull of gravity and a lot of other natural laws.

When the aria finally ended, Mom and I applauded and cheered while Daddy bowed his way over to the stereo and turned it off. In the sudden silence that followed, we all watched intently as the arm of the phonograph lifted itself from the record and clicked into place on its stand. Mom sighed. Daddy's face fell, the lines around his mouth deepening as if he were suddenly exhausted by his efforts to keep the party lively. We all went to bed early.

Friday and Saturday were cold and gray, but Sunday morning, I slept late and awoke to a sun-drenched room and something wriggling on top of my blanket. Squinting against the glare from my window—and wondering who'd dared to open those blinds—I made out the form of a . . . a cocker spaniel puppy on my bed! Daddy was leaning against my bureau, arms folded across his chest, sunshine glinting on his bald spot, a huge smile spread across his face.

"Shhhhh," he said, scooping up the puppy before my mind could even form the words to question it and signaling me to follow him.

"Where did it come from?" I whispered to him in the hall.

"Shhhhh," was all he would say.

At the end of the hall he edged open his bedroom door and we inched across the carpet to where Mom was sleeping, one hand tucked under her head, blankets up to her chin. Daddy plopped the puppy at the foot of the bed. Immediately it scrambled over to Mom and began snuffling around her ear. Her scream sent it dancing backward across the bed.

"What in the world?" Mom gasped, sitting up and groping for her glasses on the night table. *"What in the world?"*

"It's your new son," Daddy told her.

"My nuisance," Mom replied. The puppy had already forgotten its scare and was scratching what was probably a flea bite. I prayed the flea would stay out of Mom's way.

"Can we keep him, Mom? Please?" I begged.

Mom looked from me to Daddy to the puppy and back again, then smiled ruefully. "Sure, sure," she said, "as much as we can keep anything."

2

"Hi, Heather! How was your weekend?" Cara asked, dashing toward me from her house across the street for our daily trek to school.

"We got a dog," I announced. "The most adorable tan cocker spaniel puppy with ears down to the ground and these great big brown eyes. He's supposed to take Eddie's place in Mom's heart."

"You're kidding."

"Kind of. But he is supposed to cheer her up. That's why Daddy got him. Thanksgiving was rough with half the family gone."

Cara and I fell into step, our strides perfectly matched from years of marching through life side by side. We were each other's very first friends, all the way back in our diaper days.

"Your dad is so sweet," Cara commented wistfully. Her parents had gotten divorced when she was a baby. Her mother once commented that "Cara was a mistake I'm glad I made." Unlike a lot of mothers, Liz Dale will tell you stuff like that. "The wedding was for my parents," she'd gone on. "The divorce was for me." Cara sees her dad now and then, but always comes home depressed and complaining that they never have much to say to each other. "Funny," Liz commented one day, "he and I never had much to say to each other either. That's probably why we ended up with you!"

"Daddy's special, all right," I agreed as Cara and I slid across a patch of ice at the bottom of our driveway. "It's like he knows what Mom and I are thinking. He knows what we're feeling and what to do about it without our even asking. Like the puppy. Who would have guessed that what we all needed right now was a puppy? But we did."

"That's really nice. What'd you name it?"

"Daddy suggested Eddie Junior, but Mom failed to see the humor in that. She decided to call him Dandy."

"Oh, that's cute!" Cara cried.

I couldn't be entirely sure if she meant the puppy's name or the guy in the red Corvette idling at the traffic light straight ahead of us. She was talking to me, but she was looking his way. And he, of course, was looking hers. Most boys do.

Cara is not your classic beauty. Once, when we were up in my bedroom, elbow-deep in cosmetics we'd lugged home from the mall, she described herself as "a little too much of everything: a little too tall, a little too fat, a little too busty, a little too loud." It shocked me to hear her say that. As far as I'm concerned, everything she is fits together just right and always has. Girls like her because she's nice and not so gorgeous she's threatening. Boys like her. Period.

"So what's the plan of attack today?" she asked, refocusing on me as the Corvette burned rubber charging across the intersection. "We've got less than two weeks until the Snow Ball. You are running out of time."

"Maybe I just won't go," I muttered, hitching up my armload of books.

"Of course you'll go. You'll go with Nicky Simpson or you'll go stag, but you'll go."

"I'm not going stag and that's final."

"Oh, Heather, why not? I am."

"Of course you are. You can count on sixty million guys asking you to dance. I'm not going through another nightmare like Homecoming. I mean it, Cara."

"It's not as if he danced with anyone else at Homecoming."

"That is not a great comfort. You told me to wink at him across the gym, but he never so much as glanced my way, so what was I supposed to wink at? You told me to stand next to him before the music began. I stood next to him. The music began and he walked away. You told me to ask *him* to dance. By the time I'd worked up the nerve, he'd gone home. What's wrong with him, Cara? What's wrong with me?"

"He's shy. You're stubborn."

"What do you mean, I'm stubborn?"

"You could just take my advice and ask him to the Snow Ball."

"Sure, at gunpoint."

"Other girls do it. Nobody cares anymore."

Confronted with another red light, Cara and I moved sideways to wait in a sunnier spot.

"I care," I insisted. "I can't risk the rejection. Dreaming about Nicky Simpson keeps me going from day to day. Granted, he hasn't given me a lot of encouragement, but there's never been a flat-out no, either. One flat-out no and I'm left with nothing, not even the dream. I can't take that chance. At least not until we've exhausted every other possibility."

"We've come close," Cara pointed out, starting across the street. "Oh, I know what! How about we do it like we used to in junior high? I'll go over and ask him if he likes you. Remember? We used to do that to guys all the time."

"Absolutely not! Besides, he doesn't even know me."

"So I'll point you out. It'll be my chance to tell him who you are. 'See the tall, dark, and skinny one over there,' I'll say—"

"*No!* I forbid you to do that, Cara Dale."

"Okay, then, I'll ask him if he likes you and he'll say, 'I don't know. Who is she?' and I'll say, 'I'm sorry, but I'm not at liberty to divulge that information. However, if you will stand at the corner of Twelfth and Vine at precisely six P.M. . . .' "

"Come on, Cara, get serious."

"I'm running out of ideas, Heather."

"You? Never. When it comes to boys, you have one of the great creative minds of this century."

"And you have one of the great leftover minds from the last century. For the last time, Heather, ask him to the dance."

"For the last time, Cara, no. Either he asks me, or . . ."

"Or what?"

"Or . . . or we have until the Sweetheart Ball in February to try again. Or the Spring Fling in May." Lucky for me, our PTA loves to sponsor dances. They raise lots of money and keep us kids off the street. There's not a lot to do in this town.

"Aaaaaagh, I can't stand it," Cara wailed, then threw me an exasperated glance and began to laugh.

I chuckled along, but the situation was slightly less humorous from my point of view. I'd been trying to get Nicky Simpson to notice me since September. I'd done

everything I could think of, short of tap-dancing on top
of his desk. What was I, the Invisible Woman?

Cara and I entered the ancient pile of red brick
known as Hanover High through a basement door that
led past the gym locker rooms, through a long, narrow
hallway to the lunchroom, and beyond that to our street
lockers. Juniors and seniors had lockers on the first floor;
freshmen and sophomores, in the basement. It was an
old Hanover High tradition. Another old Hanover High
tradition was to get your stuff into and out of your
locker and your body up to the first floor while the
junior and senior guys were still at *their* lockers.

As usual, while we made our way down the tunnel-
like hall, boys heading the other way toward gym did
cute little things when they saw Cara—bobbing and
feinting in front of her as if they weren't going to let her
pass, clever stuff like that. At least ten guys go through
that exact same routine every day.

Cara responded with her standard giggles and dim-
ples. "Kevin! Tommy!" she squealed, sidestepping one
goofy admirer after another. "Oh, come on, Bert. Very
funny, Stu. Michael, quit that!"

As each boy's name was called, he flushed with pride
as if he were Cara's one and only favorite. How she
made them all feel that way at once, I never have figured out.

Suddenly a commotion broke out up the hall and
everybody pressed themselves flat against the tiles. In
the next instant Vice-Principal Hutton's voice boomed
down the tunnel like a subway train hooting its arrival.
Then he appeared, preceded by a miserable-looking kid
whose collar he was mashing in his beefy ex-halfback's
paw.

"If I ever catch you doing anything like that again,

Jackson," he roared, "I'll have you in juvenile court so fast it'll make your head swim. Got it?"

"Yeah," Jackson whimpered, dancing up the hall between two lines of wide-eyed spectators like a puppet caught on tangled strings.

"What'd you say?"

"Yes, sir, Mr. Hutton," Jackson croaked, his cheeks blotched red in embarrassment and mortal fear.

At this point they were almost in front of me. Even though I wasn't the one in trouble, my knees were shaking from the sheer force of Mr. Hutton's fury. Then, over Jackson's bobbing blond head, I caught Mr. Hutton's eye. For just a fraction of a second, it twinkled and the merest hint of a smile wriggled at the corner of his mouth.

"That's better," he barked at Jackson, releasing his collar with a forward thrust to hasten him on down the hall. In their wake eyes rolled, shoulders hunched, and the two streams of traffic continued on their way in sudden, thunderstruck silence.

"I think you just saved Jackson's life," Cara said when we were far enough away to breathe freely again.

"What are you talking about?"

"I saw the little smile between you and Mr. Hutton. And how he calmed down right after."

"You're crazy."

"Oh, no, I'm not. Older men like you. Mr. Allison liked you in algebra, and not just because you have a way with equations. You were even Mr. Collier's pet back in fourth grade, and he hated everybody. Older men recognize your qualities."

"Wonderful," I said. "Maybe Santa Claus will ask me to the Snow Ball."

"You're what my mom calls a late bloomer," Cara

went on, an index finger tapping the air to emphasize her point. "Not what the average high school flibbertigibbet is looking for. Don't worry, though—"

My elbow hit her rib cage just in time to choke off the rest of her statement. Before she could protest, Nicky Simpson crossed our path, then slipped noiselessly up the stairs and out of sight, dark and elusive as a Halloween cat.

"He is not the average high school flibbertigibbet," I said. "I'm *exactly* what he's looking for. *I* know it. Why doesn't *he*?"

3

I have only one class with Nicky Simpson, geometry. It was there that I noticed him on the first day of school, seated in the first seat of the first row, the one nearest the door, chewing the eraser off his pencil and looking as if he'd rather be anywhere else in the world but there. One glimpse of the way his dark hair flopped over his forehead, almost obscuring his dark, brooding eyes, and I was glad to see him exactly where he was.

Cara and I had chosen seats in the middle of the room, in what we'd once determined was every teacher's blind spot, the area where students were least often called upon when not volunteering.

"He's mine," I'd said, nodding in Nicky's direction as I moved my desk and chair a bit closer to Cara's.

"Who is he?"

"Haven't the slightest idea, but he's mine."

"Why, Heather Connelly, has a prince finally crashed through the thicket to awaken Sleeping Beauty? What has this guy got that the thousands you've ignored were missing?"

"Me," I'd said. Only, as it turned out, I was the one

who had to go crashing through the thicket, and the prince was one sound sleeper.

He was new in town, he came from Kansas City, he was a sophomore, and he drove a battered blue Dodge Dart. That was all I had been able to find out about him. Most people hadn't even noticed him, and he seemed to be doing his best to keep it that way.

Oh, and he ruined a lot of perfectly good pencils by chewing off their erasers prematurely. Not a major piece of information, perhaps, but still the kind of tidbit I'd been living on for months. He was destroying his latest as Cara and I approached geometry class that Monday after Thanksgiving. Suddenly, Cara laid a hand on my arm and drew me back to where we couldn't be seen from inside the classroom.

"He's working on our assignment for today," she hissed. "He must be having trouble with it."

"How do you know?"

"He's got his book open to the page with that rotten trapezoid, he's deep in thought, and the assignment's due in five minutes. Go offer to help him."

"Are you crazy?"

"I will be if you don't take advantage of this golden opportunity. I mean it, Heather, get in there and *talk to him.*"

It was not a totally ridiculous idea. After all, I told myself, I am good at math. I pictured our heads close together as we analyzed an intriguing formula or two. Stomach quaking, I slipped into the seat behind his. Mrs. Ridling, our teacher, glanced up from her desk, then went back to grading papers. Geometry was our first class of the day, and the bell had not yet rung.

"Having trouble with the assignment?" I asked, voice rasping through constricted throat. I was doing it! I was talking to Nicky Simpson. Three months of effort had brought me to this!

He spun around, brown eyes regarding me with mild surprise.

"No," he said.

My mouth fell open. My eyes darted toward Cara, already seated two rows away. She clapped one hand across her grin and quickly lowered her head over her own book. I turned back toward Nicky, my cheeks ablaze.

"Oh," I said. "I thought maybe you were." There was a long and horrible pause. "Sorry," I mumbled at last, and somehow managed to slither away to my regular seat beside Cara.

"Sorry," she whispered.

"A flat-out no," I moaned.

That afternoon I was scheduled to work in Mr. Hutton's office. Three days a week, instead of going to study hall, I answer his phone, run errands, and so on, while his secretary goes to lunch. Still mulling over my humiliation in geometry, I dropped my books on Mrs. Till's desk and was just getting settled in her chair when Mr. Hutton emerged from the crowd passing in the hallway.

"Nothing much doing today, sunshine," he said. "I'll be back in a few minutes. Hold down the fort."

The next thing I knew, he was gone and Nicky Simpson had taken his place in the doorway. He seemed very tall from my seated position, tall and lanky and not terribly well cared for. One side of his shirt collar was sticking out of his sweater, the other was tucked in, and the whole outfit could have done with a pressing. There was enough of Mom in me to make me want to take him in hand and tidy him up.

"Hi," he said.

"Hi," I said.

"For Mr. Hutton," he said, handing me a manila envelope. "Stuff from my old school."

"I'll see that he gets it."

"Thank you," he said, and left.

Our second conversation, another spellbinder.

Two weeks passed, Friday of the Snow Ball arrived, and no more progress had been made. As it turned out, Cara didn't go to the dance either. She and her mom left that morning to spend the holidays in New York with relatives. She missed the last few days of school before Christmas break. So did I, but for a very different reason.

I plodded home from school Snow Ball Friday under a sky as dismal as my mood. With Cara gone, I was left to argue on all alone: Maybe I should have asked Nicky to the dance. Or maybe I should just give up. A note was waiting for me on the kitchen counter.

"Heather—I'm at the supermarket. Daddy's napping upstairs, so be quiet, okay? Be back soon. Love, Mom. P.S. Keep an eye on Dandy."

Dandy was nowhere to be seen, so I hung my coat in the closet and tiptoed upstairs, wondering why Daddy was home from work so early and napping. The master bedroom door was slightly ajar. I poked my nose in.

"That your nose, Heather?" Daddy asked.

Chuckling, I pushed the door open and went inside. Daddy was stretched out on top of the flowered bedspread, looking pale against its ruddy tones. Dandy, curled up in the crook of his arm, ears neatly spread out to either side of his droopy face, gave me a puppy smile as I sat down on Mom's side of the bed.

"How come you're home?" I asked Daddy.

"Feelin' a mite puny, as they say. Accounted for one too many accounts, I suppose."

Daddy is a certified public accountant, which is probably why I'm so good at math.

"How did your day go?" he asked, rubbing the sleep from his eyes.

I gathered Dandy up in my arms before answering. "It wasn't horrible or anything," I began, "but . . ."

"But what?"

"It was discouraging. They all are, lately."

Daddy—and Dandy—eyed me with interest. "How so?" Daddy asked.

"You really want to hear about it?"

"Of course I do. If you really want to tell me."

"I do . . . but it's kind of dumb."

"What a coincidence! I've been in the mood for dumb all week." He pushed himself to a sitting position, back against the headboard, ready to listen.

"Okay," I said, smiling in spite of feeling silly, and out poured the whole dumb story of Nicky Simpson— who would not ask me to dance, who needed no help in math, who paid more attention to the erasers on his pencils than to me. Daddy took in the whole ridiculous tale without interrupting. "Why is it so hard for me and so easy for Cara?" I asked, at last.

"Probably because you're you and Cara's Cara."

"What's that supposed to mean?"

"It means small talk and flirting and being a social butterfly come naturally to some people, but not to others. Some of us tend to take life more slowly, more seriously, perhaps. Look at me, for instance. Had my nose buried in a book from kindergarten through graduate school."

"The same book?" I asked, suddenly feeling less intense about everything.

"Of course," Daddy said, laughing. "I was a very slow reader. Seriously, I never got the hang of dating, never.

Then one day I saw your mother, and I've been the happiest person on Earth ever since."

"That's odd," I said. "One day I saw Nicky, and I've been the most miserable person on Earth ever since." I glanced down at Dandy, who'd dozed off in my arms. "You don't think it's a fault?" I asked. "There's not something missing inside of me?"

Daddy reached over and absently flipped Dandy's ear while considering his answer. Without waking, Dandy twitched the ear back into place. "If you never loved *anybody*," Daddy said slowly, "then I'd worry. But I don't see where that could possibly be a problem in your case."

"You're sure?" I asked, realizing the answer in advance as my love for him swelled my heart.

Daddy grinned. "Bank on it," he said, "and we accountants don't say those words lightly."

With that he swung his feet over the edge of the bed and stood up. Suddenly a shadow crossed his face, but before I could ask what was wrong, it had passed and he was putting on his jacket. Dandy bounced off my lap and followed him to the door.

"I'm going to visit Uncle Will," Daddy announced. "I won't be long."

"Want me to come?"

The question had a childish ring to it, an echo of all the eager trips to Uncle Will's house when Eddie and I were little and couldn't wait to see what wooden train or horse or intricate puzzle was waiting for us in his garage workshop. Sawdust was our favorite smell back then. "Your daddy got your grandma's brains," Uncle Will would say, "but I got your grandpa's magic fingers."

I never knew my grandparents, and yet I feel as if I

did, because Uncle Will kept them alive for me. Now I miss them and him too, the person he was before the strokes, the hospital, and the nursing home.

"There's no need for you to come," Daddy said, "but thank you for asking." He came back for a quick hug and then headed for the stairs. "Better put Dandy in the yard," he called over his shoulder, "before he mistakes our rug for grass."

Too late.

4

Mom arrived home as I was scrubbing at the stain in her rug with a rag soaked in ammonia. I sheepishly waved the rag in greeting as she came through the bedroom door.

"Oh, no, not again," she cried, taking the rag from my hand for a few expert swipes at the damage.

"You mean he's done it up here before?" I asked.

"Of course he has. Even though I've begged your father not to let him upstairs. If it were up to me, he wouldn't even be in the house."

"Oh, Mom, how can you resist? Dandy's too cute to keep outside *all* the time."

"I can resist. Believe me, I can resist. With every puddle, I can resist a little better." She went into the bathroom off her bedroom to dispose of the rag. "Where'd your father go?" she asked, her voice raised over running water.

"To visit Uncle Will."

The faucets squealed shut and Mom reappeared in the bathroom doorway. "You're kidding," she said.

"No, I'm not. That's where he went. What's wrong?"

"Nothing. Nothing at all. Finish rinsing out that rag and hang it on the back porch. I've got to start dinner."

Something was wrong, all right, but I didn't find out what until just before dinner, and even then I didn't realize its seriousness. I was on my way downstairs to feed Dandy when I heard Mom's raised voice through the closed kitchen door.

"You're exhausted," she was saying. "You were restless all night. I'll tell you something, Bernie. I wish you'd retire."

"I'm only fifty-one years old," I heard Daddy say, amusement in his voice in spite of the anger in Mom's. "Besides, how would we live?"

"We'd live. Somehow. Maybe we couldn't have everything we have now, but we'd live. There's plenty we could do without. I'd gladly do without lots of things so you'd never have to see that partner of yours again."

"Joe? Joe's all right."

"He's not all right and you know it. The bigger your business grows, the crazier he gets. He thinks everybody in the world is just waiting to grab it all away from him. You, in particular."

"That's not so. We've been friends all our lives."

"*You've* been a friend. Not him. Oh, what's the use of talking? The problem can be staring you right in the face and you refuse to see it. You've never said a word against him and you never will."

"I don't like to cause trouble."

"No, you don't. Instead you get high blood pressure. Instead you don't sleep at night. And then you drag yourself out of bed when you should be resting to see a brother who doesn't even know you're there."

"You worry about me too much," Daddy said lightly. "A casual observer might conclude that you love me."

"Sure, sure, I love you," I heard Mom mutter. I could imagine Daddy sidling up to give her a peck on the cheek and Mom's stern expression melting into a smile. I waited a minute or two before pushing through the swinging door. Sure enough, they were at the stove, standing very close together.

"Takes two to boil spaghetti?" I asked.

Daddy winked. "Feed your precious dog," Mom said.

When I came down to breakfast that Monday morning, Daddy had already left for work.

"Early," Mom muttered, drying dishes with a vengeance, "so he can squeeze in a few more hours of aggravation."

A few more hours was all he had. I took the call myself that afternoon in Mr. Hutton's office. Odd thing about that day: I remember so vividly everything that happened before Mom's call, and so dimly whatever followed it.

It was such an *ordinary* morning: I left for school. I spent first hour staring morosely at the back of Nicky Simpson's head. I wandered from class to class, smiling, waving, chatting—all the while storing up the best of my lovelorn despair for Cara's return from New York. I reported for duty in Mr. Hutton's office, hoping as usual that Nicky would have another errand to run in that direction, something terribly complicated that would plunge us into Conversation Three.

A perfectly normal day—and then the phone rang.

"This is Mrs. Connelly," I heard Mom say. "I'd like to speak to my daughter, Heather."

"Mom? Hi! This is me."

"Heather? Come home," she said. Then I heard her draw her breath in sharply. "It's your father."

"What is it?" I asked. "What's wrong?"

"I . . . I'm . . . Heather, he's dead."

Just like that. Just words, two words, and the world cracked open, pieces falling through space. I didn't even realize I was crying until Mr. Hutton took the receiver from my hand and hung up the phone.

"He's dead. My father's dead," I told him. He knelt beside the chair, put my head on his shoulder and let me cry.

Daddy had collapsed at his office and died in the ambulance on the way to the hospital. "He was all alone" were Mom's first words when Mr. Hutton brought me home. There'd been paramedics in the ambulance, of course, but I knew what she meant.

I was okay at the funeral—as long as the coffin stayed open. Daddy didn't really seem gone. He was right there in front of me, dressed in his best suit, a gray pinstripe. He'd bought it to wear to my cousin Betty's wedding. It was expensive, more than he'd ever spent on himself before, and it made him look fine. The day he got it, he'd put it on and strutted around the living room so proudly, Mom and I had laughed. At the wedding he'd danced all the slow dances with Mom, except one, which he'd danced with me, humming softly against my hair. Could that have been only four months ago? Above my head the service droned on as I counted: September . . . October . . . November . . . December. He was wearing the suit now for the second time.

An attendant in a white uniform took Mom's arm and helped her to her feet. Nudged from the other side by Eddie, I stood up and followed them. We passed Daddy, then left him behind as we entered a small waiting room beside the chapel. It didn't seem right to leave him like that. He looked so vulnerable, so alone. I was seized by an urge to hold him close, to protect him from this strange and terrible thing that was happening.

The waiting-room door closed behind us. Mom sat

stiffly on the edge of a beige sofa, her hands folded in her lap, eyes moist and vague beneath the veil of her little black hat. Marie sat down beside her and put an arm around her shoulders, but Mom didn't seem to notice. Then Eddie knelt and covered Mom's hands with his.

"Mom," he said, huskily, "I just want to—"

"Don't!" Mom cried, pulling her hands back as if they'd been burned. "Please don't talk about it. Don't."

Eddie looked up at me in confusion, but all I could do was shake my head and shrug. Daddy would have known what to do for her. . . .

The wrinkled face of the attendant passed before me as she once again cupped Mom's elbow in her waxy, freckled hand and led us all back into the chapel.

The coffin was closed.

5

Choking on tears, I sat up in bed. The room was dark
except for a pale ribbon of moonlight across my desk
and door. I rubbed my aching eyes and wiped the tears
from my cheeks with my pajama sleeves. I'd been
dreaming about the funeral. I dreamed about it every
night for days after it happened. In my dream the coffin
lid was still open as they lowered Daddy into the
ground. High above his serene face, I stood sobbing.
And then he woke up! Magically, he stood beside me
and held me in his arms; he rocked me and whispered
that everything was all right. I could smell the newness
of his suit and feel its prickly texture against my cheek.
He wasn't really dead at all. There was no such thing as
death. He promised to stay with me, to never, ever leave.

Each night I woke up almost convinced that if I believed hard enough, if I held on to the dream tightly
enough, I could make it come true.

Nutty though it was, I had to get out of bed, cross the
hall, and peek into Mom's room. He was not sleeping
there, flat on his back with his right arm tucked behind
his head, breath coming in low, rhythmic snores like the

deepest purring of a satisfied cat. He would not come to the breakfast table in the morning in shirt sleeves and tie, bringing with him the sweet sting of aftershave— and a fresh supply of awful jokes. "Did you know orange juice was named after a famous athlete?" A giggle caught in my throat even as fresh tears formed rivulets down my cheeks.

I padded downstairs. The house seemed airless and empty, even with Dandy thumping and whining on the other side of the kitchen door. I unhooked the latch Daddy had installed for the sake of peace between Mom and Dandy and gathered his sleep-warmed little body into my arms.

In the first few days after the funeral, my nightly wanderings had found filled ashtrays and emptied coffee mugs everywhere, left by the crowd of family and friends who had come to visit. All day long, people had bustled in and out, mostly women Mom knew from her volunteer work, toting baskets of fruit, cake, pots of coffee, filling the house with perfume, smoke, and chatter. Mom, the tiny dark center of attention seated on the sofa, gossiped and smiled and only now and then grew misty-eyed as reality wedged its way through chinks in the wall of friendship. She kept offering to make herself useful, and they kept insisting she just relax and let them take care of everything. "I don't want to be a burden," I heard her say.

Somehow we got through Christmas. New Year's Eve came and went quietly. The ashtrays and mugs stayed clean and stacked in the cupboard, Eddie and Marie went back to Oregon, the last of the fruit rattled around in our refrigerator bin, and it seemed as if Mom, Dandy, and I were suddenly alone on the planet, as if we'd been cut adrift from life itself.

A blast of cold air hit me as I opened the back door to let Dandy out into the yard. He tried to slip back into the kitchen between my legs, but I caught him and set him firmly on the porch, closing the door behind him. I pressed my forehead against the cold pane and watched him sniff the frozen ground for an appropriate stopping place. In seconds he was finished and yapping to be let back in.

I tucked him inside my robe and went into the living room. Curled up in Daddy's corner of the sofa, we both managed to fall asleep for another hour or so, until the sounds of Mom puttering around upstairs woke us up. Slowly unwinding my stiff limbs, I wondered how I would ever stay awake in school, and then marveled at how oddly removed school life seemed from this new existence without Daddy. I gave Dandy his morning Puppy Chow and milk and brought the paper inside.

"You slept?" Mom asked, coming into the kitchen minutes later and surprising me in the middle of Ann Landers.

"Uh-huh." No sense mentioning how poorly.

I slipped the local section out of the folded paper and passed it to Mom across the glass tabletop. We read, nibbled toast, and sipped coffee quietly, separate as strangers sharing a table in a restaurant. We were up too early for the usual panic and confusion of rushing me off to school—and Daddy off to work. It left us at a loss for getting the day's conversation started.

"Good sales at the mall today," I observed.

"Hmmmm. Going to be a little warmer than yester-day."

It was more than a lack of morning things to talk about. Since Daddy's death, an uneasiness had sprung up between us. Frightened at the thought, I was seized by an urge to *move*. I jumped to my feet and announced that I was going upstairs to get dressed. Mom nodded absently, adjusting her glasses for a better view of the paper. I took off for my room and closed the door.

A photograph of Daddy, young and handsome in his army uniform, smiled up at me from my bureau. I'd found it when Eddie, Marie, and I were cleaning out his closet after the funeral and claimed it for my own. I couldn't look at it without crying, but that didn't keep me from looking at it now. Finally I put it down and was headed for a shower when the phone rang.

"I'll get it!" I yelled, and made a dash for the extension next to Mom's bed. "Hello?"

"Hi. I'm home."

"Cara?"

"Yes, we're back. Oh, Heather, I'm so sorry about your father. I feel awful that we weren't here."

"It's all right. You couldn't have known."

"My mom said to tell your mom she'll stop by right after work. We got in late last night or she would've called."

"Okay, I'll tell her."

"He was very, very special."

"Yes." Tears swelled my throat painfully. To keep them back, I changed the subject. "How was your trip?"

"Really nice. The Big Apple—if you don't look too closely—is heaven."

"I want to hear all about it."

"I want to tell you all about it. Are you going to school?"

"Sure."

"Great. Your porch, eight thirty?"

"I'll be there. Bye."

My path crossed Mom's in the hall. "That was Cara,"

I announced. "Her mom said to tell you she'd be over to see you after work."

"Oh? To see *me*?"

"Yes. You know . . . because of Daddy."

Mom stiffened, as if it hurt her physically to hear me say his name. I remembered her plea to Eddie at the funeral and resolved not to do it again.

6

"You sure you want to hear about New York right now?" Cara asked. She'd greeted me on our front porch with a squeal, a bear hug, and a kiss that had missed my cheek and knocked my earmuffs askew. Then she'd pulled back, blue eyes clouded with sympathy.

"Yes," I insisted. "I really do."

"Well . . . I got drunk."

"What?"

Grabbing my elbow, she hustled me down the steps and aimed us toward school. "You heard me. I got drunk. Bombed. *Wasted.*"

"You're kidding. Where?"

"In New York. In a bar. With my cousins."

"I thought you had to be eighteen to drink in New York."

"Nope. You just have to *look* eighteen. I knew all this extra blubber would come in handy one day."

"You don't have any extra blubber," I said, by force of habit. Cara doesn't wear glasses, but I swear there's something wrong with her eyes. She really thinks she's fat. Her corneas must be shaped like funhouse mirrors.

"Okay," she agreed reluctantly, "but I am mature for my age. Ask any bartender."

"What was it like? What were you drinking?"

"Manhattans, naturally. The first one tasted like gasoline. The second one tasted pretty good. The third one tasted even better. And the fourth one I threw up for half an hour in the ladies' room."

"Oh, Cara, you're too much. Did your mom find out?"

"Of course. She got back to my aunt's house a little after we did. I was lying awake in the dark, watching the room spin. My cousin Davey told me it'd stop if I kept one foot on the floor, but when I tried that, I fell out of bed. That's when my mom found out."

"What'd she say?"

"She laughed and said I'd gotten exactly what I deserved."

"Your mom's terrific," I said.

"Oh, sure. Terrific," Cara echoed dryly.

I waited, eyebrows raised, for an explanation, but Cara ignored me and trudged on, suddenly lost in thought. Half a block later I decided I'd better break into her mood. No sense starting the week off in a funk, no matter what the cause.

"You're getting too far ahead of me," I said. "First boys, now alcohol. You're going to drive first, too. And lose your virginity first, for sure. I can't keep up. You're going to outgrow me. You'll have to give me away, like last year's coat."

"Never," Cara responded, her quick smile back in place. "I'll keep you hanging at the back of my closet for old times' sake."

"Gee, thanks."

"Tell you what, just for you I'll give up drinking for a while. Unless I can order only second and third drinks.

Everything before and after is truly disgusting, not to mention untidy. As for boys, I suppose you managed not to go to the Snow Ball?"

"You suppose right."

"I'm not giving up boys, Heather. Either you make your move soon, or it's the back of the closet for you."

By a strange quirk of fate, it was neither. A lot of people stopped me in school that day to say they were sorry about my father. One of them was Nicky Simpson.

It happened after geometry. Cara and I had gathered our books and were almost out the door when I felt a hand on my shoulder. I spun around to find Nicky staring down at me, looking every bit as shocked by his action as I felt.

"I—uh—I read about your dad," he stammered. "In the paper. I'm sorry. Must have been a rotten Christmas for you."

I was so surprised, I didn't have time or room inside to feel nervous, at least not immediately.

"My brother and sister-in-law were here," I said. "That helped. But thank you. I didn't know . . . you knew . . . I mean, who I was . . . even." I looked to Cara for support as my voice retreated down my throat.

"Excuse me," she said, "I'm going to check my locker for fleas."

It was not a graceful exit. It left Nicky and me blushing. But smiling.

"I've got study hall next hour," he said. "Can I walk you to your next class?"

"It's all the way in the basement. I've got gym."

"That's okay. Brownstein never takes roll. Half our study hall comes in late and the other half never shows up."

So there we were, Nicky Simpson and I, strolling

down the hall side by side. Very strange, and getting stranger.

"I—uh—I know who you are, all right," he said. "You've been trying to . . . to be nice, and . . . I haven't . . . um, well, I guess I've been pretty stupid about it all. But—well, I didn't—never mind. I went to the Snow Ball thinking you'd be there."

"Did you really?"

"Uh-huh."

"I stayed home, thinking you wouldn't be there."

"Oh, God. Well, serves me right, I guess. It's all on account of—well, never mind."

I was dying to know what lay behind the "never minds," but I knew better than to ask. We were in the tunnel now, forced into single file by the traffic moving both ways. Nicky had to walk backward so we could still talk.

"Your address was in the paper. You practically live on the other side of town from me, you know that? Lucky I have a car."

"I don't even have my license. I won't be sixteen for two more months."

"I got mine last fall. Got the car then, too. Paid for it myself, with my life savings. I figured out the bus route, too, from my house to yours. In this crazy town, I'd have to change lines. It'd take me about an hour. I could walk it faster."

"You figured out the bus route?"

"Yeah. Before I'd even said hello. Actually, I knew your address before it was in the paper. Pretty crazy, huh?"

We'd come out of the tunnel and were standing in front of the door to the girls' locker room. Nicky shifted uncomfortably from one foot to the other, and gazed

around as if the next thing to say might be written on a
cue card somewhere.

"Not as crazy as you'd think," I told him. "Well,
crazy, but not unheard of. I've known your address a
long time, too."

Nicky laughed and ran his fingers through the hair
falling in his eyes. I fought the urge to help him pat it
gently into place. "One of us should have spent less time
in the phone book and more on the phone," he observed.
I nodded in agreement. We took some time to ruminate
on that point, while smiling foolishly. "Well," Nicky
said, breathing the word out hard and gesturing toward
the locker room door. "Guess this is as far as I can go."

"Guess so," I said, taking my time in the doorway.

"You missed a lot of school before Christmas," he
pointed out, suddenly speaking very quickly. "Maybe I
could come over tonight and help you catch up in geometry."

"I'd like that." The understatement of the century.

"Okay. I'll call you after dinner."

"Great. Thanks."

Sporting a grin that was threatening to swell out of
control and swallow up my head, I backed through the
doorway into the locker room, trampled on Cara's
sneakered foot, and turned my ankle.

"Ouch!" we cried in unison. Then "Shhhhh!" we
hissed at each other, afraid that Nicky was still close
enough to hear. Cara hopped over and closed the door,
then we leaned against the brick wall side by side, mas-
saging our injured parts and alternating fits of laughter
with groans of pain.

"How long have you been standing there?" I asked
her.

"Long enough. In fact, so long we'll both be late for
class. You better get a move on."

I limped across the room to my locker. "I can't believe this is happening," I said, tearing at the buttons on my shirt. "How can one half of me be so happy while the other half is still sad? I feel like my brain is going to explode."

"If you don't get suited up in a hurry, we get ten laps around the gym," Cara pointed out. "That ought to clear your head."

We got ten laps around the gym. I didn't mind; the steady jogging pace gave me time to think. It didn't seem right, somehow, that Daddy's death should bring Nicky and me together. On the other hand, why question a miracle? And Mom was getting on with her life. She'd returned to her volunteer work at the hospital and was even talking about evening classes at the university and finding a job. Somehow all her hustle and bustle didn't seem quite right to me either, but if it worked for her, if it made her happy, who was I to cast doubt?

I got all kinds of homework done that night, leaving geometry for last. Dinner passed, then seven o'clock, then eight. Nicky did call, finally, but only to tell me he wouldn't be over.

"I'm sorry," he said, with what sounded more like anger than regret. "There's a lot of stuff I have to do around the house. Chapters Ten, Eleven, and Twelve, that's what you missed. They're not too tough."

"I'll manage, I guess," I said.

"Yeah. Well. See you tomorrow."

I'd barely hung up when the phone rang again. It was Cara.

"Has he called yet? I've been watching your driveway, but no Dodge Dart. What's up?"

"He just called. He's not coming."

"Why not?"

"I don't know. Some stuff he has to do at home."

"Ah, that's too bad. But he did call. That's encouraging."

"Mmmmmph."

"Now, now, don't give up on him. If at first you don't

succeed, eat something. How does chocolate cake sound?"

"What are you talking about?"

"Food. My mom wanted to invite you and your mom over for dessert tonight. First I told her you couldn't, but now I see you can. How about it?"

"Sure, why not. I'll ask."

I left the phone dangling and dashed upstairs to knock on Mom's bathroom door. "Want to go over to the Dales' house for a while?" I yelled.

I could hear bath water sloshing.

"Hello in there?" I called, rapping louder.

The sloshing stopped. "What? Did you call me?"

"Yes. Cara just phoned and asked us over for dessert."

Soft thuds and squishy sounds meant Mom was climbing out of the tub. A moment later she opened the door a crack, her chenille robe clutched to her throat, steam billowing up behind her. The aroma of lavender tickled my nose.

"What happened to that fellow—Nicky?" she asked.

"He can't make it. So let's go to Cara's, okay?" I said quickly, not wanting to linger on my disappointment.

Mom gave it a moment's thought. "I don't think so," she said. "I had a long day at the hospital and I'm going back tomorrow. I think I'd better get to bed early."

"You only go Mondays, Wednesdays, and Fridays," I said. "Tomorrow's Tuesday."

"I'm learning the dispatcher's job," she explained. "She's quitting and it looks like I'm up for it."

"That's wonderful," I said, "but why didn't you tell me before?"

Mom works for Home Meals, a project that delivers hot lunches to the housebound and people on welfare. Everyone involved is a volunteer, except the dispatcher, who coordinates everything and works every day. As organized as Mom is, she'd be perfect for the job.

"It all came up suddenly," she explained, "and nothing's certain until I get through a couple of interviews tomorrow. You go on to Cara's. Don't stay too late. Wish me luck and a good night's sleep."

Before I could wish her anything, she'd closed the door, leaving behind only a lavender mist. It was only eight thirty. How much sleep could two interviews take?

"One Connelly's better than none," Cara announced, leading me into the kitchen, where her mom was setting out plates, "and means more chocolate cake for me. Eight hundred and ninety-three calories per slice, recipe imported directly from New York, baked and pretested by your own chubby pal."

"You're not chubby," Liz Dale and I responded in unison.

"Good," said Cara. "Then let's eat."

"You girls eat," Liz said. "I think I'll pass. Unless you need my help?"

"Oh, no, we'll manage fine," Cara told her while lifting something huge and deeply chocolate out of the refrigerator.

"I thought so," Liz said, sending a wink my way. She left the kitchen with that purposeful long-legged stride Cara and I have been trying to imitate since childhood. Jane Fonda has it. Cara and I do not.

"It's got chocolate, it's got caramel, it's got nuts," Cara chanted, cutting each of us a huge portion of cake. "Isn't it wonderful?"

Mouth full, I nodded enthusiastically. We ate in worshipful silence for a while, giving each morsel our undivided attention.

"So, what's next with you and Nicky?" Cara asked at last.

"I haven't the slightest idea."

"It's only a matter of time till he asks you out."

"Maybe. Maybe not."

"You don't sound too eager."

"I'm not. I mean, I am, but it doesn't feel right. My father just died a couple of weeks ago. I'm not supposed to be having fun yet, am I?"

"Hey," Cara said softly, putting down a forkful of cake, "knowing your dad, I really don't think he'd mind."

I smiled, agreeing that Daddy probably wouldn't, but I pushed my plate aside, suddenly not hungry anymore.

"Are you all right?" Cara asked, her eyes narrowing. "I mean, you know, *really*?"

I shrugged. "I guess so," I said. "I still cry a lot, but I suppose that's what anybody would do. It just seems so . . . strange."

"How do you mean?"

"I'm not sure. It's like putting a jigsaw puzzle together, only you know there's a piece missing and you'll never be able to replace it, but you still have to make the picture come out right. I can't figure out how to do that."

We both sighed and were quiet for a moment.

"My mom said your mom's doing remarkably well," Cara said.

"She did?"

"Uh-huh. Those were her exact words."

"That's good to know. I really wasn't sure. You know my mom, she doesn't say much."

"She's never been a big talker."

"No, but . . ."

"But what?"

"Oh, nothing." It was too weird to share, even with Cara: Not only did Mom not talk about Daddy's death, she didn't even cry!

"Listen," Cara said, lowering her voice, "it can go the other way, too. Take my mom, for instance. She'll tell you more than you ever wanted to hear."

"Oh, come on, Cara, it's great to have a mother as open as yours. You can discuss *anything* with her."

"True, whether you want to or not. You think I *like* knowing I was a mistake? I could have lived quite happily without that information. She could've set her wedding date back a year; I'd never check the license."

"You'd rather she'd lied to you?"

"Well, no, I guess not. What I'm saying is, some things don't need to be shared."

That gave me a lot to think about. Privacy was what Mom seemed to want, and she was certainly entitled to it. I'd have to keep that in mind.

"You going to finish that?" Cara asked, pointing her fork at my cake.

In spite of everything, I laughed. "No."

"Waste not, want not," she said, and polished off the last few bites, as I knew she would. With a satisfied sigh she rose from her seat and carried our plates to the sink.

"Can I help?" I asked.

"Nah, it'll just take a second."

"Then I think I better go. I've still got geometry to do."

"How can I be friends with someone who puts math before chocolate cake and boys?" Cara wondered aloud.

"Opposites attract," I said. "You're blond, I'm dark."

"I'm fat, you're thin."

"For the zillionth time, Cara Dale," I intoned, "you are *not fat*. You are *just fine*. Period. Good night."

When I got home, Mom was already in bed, her lights off. Dandy had barely enough energy left for a wiggly greeting and was quickly bedded down for the night in his box by the basement door. I wished him pleasant dreams, locked up, and turned off the downstairs lights. Suddenly the house grew heavy with its own silence.

8

Nicky was not in school the next day, or for the rest of the week.

"Should I call him?" I asked Cara at least once every fifteen minutes, whether we were eating, reading, or hanging from the ropes in gym.

"Sure. Call him when you get home," she'd say.

"I can't call him."

"So don't call him."

"I feel as if I should, though. Maybe he's sick."

"So do."

"I can't."

"So don't."

"You're a very patient person, Cara," I mentioned as Friday rolled to a close and we walked home through flurries of snow.

"Not really. After a day with you, I go home, stick my head in a bucket, and scream until I pass out. After a day with you, that feels good."

"Okay, okay," I said. "I'll call him."

When I got home, Mom was running the vacuum cleaner around the living room and Dandy was hiding behind a big claw foot of the dining-room table, so scared he wagged his greeting at me without leaving his safe spot.

"Aren't you too tired for that after a day at the hospital?" I yelled at Mom over the sweeper's roar. She'd passed her interviews and had begun working eight thirty to three thirty daily.

She flipped off the power and straightened up slowly, one hand to the small of her back. "Not really," she said. "There, I sit. This is my exercise. Three days as a dispatcher and I already miss jumping in and out of the car juggling lunches. How was your day?"

"Pretty good." Taking advantage of the sudden quiet, Dandy danced up beside me, stood on his hind legs, and pawed my jeans. "Down!" I commanded. His brown eyes filled with dismay and he whined pitifully until I lifted him up and buried my cold nose in his warm fur.

"He's a genius," Mom observed. "You say down and he goes up." With a last rub to her back, she bent over toward the power switch. "Dinner will be ready at six," she added.

"You've already cooked? You don't want to eat out?"

"What for? I've got roast beef, potatoes, and spinach casserole, all your favorites."

"Wow, and here I was thinking of having a snack. I better wait."

"You can eat something. You're too thin."

"I don't want to spoil my appetite."

"You're losing weight. I don't like it."

"I'm not losing weight, *you* are."

"I can afford it. Now, eat something."

"Okay, okay." I put Dandy down and let him chase me into the kitchen. Grabbing a rawhide bone for him and a glass of milk and Oreos for me, I started back just as the vacuum cleaner roared to life again. Dandy cowered under the kitchen table.

"Oh, come on," I said. I balanced the bone, milk, and cookies in one arm and scooped him up with the other.

"I'm going upstairs," I announced to Mom. She nodded, edging one side of the sofa forward and poking at it with the vacuum cleaner rod like a tiny knight jabbing a dragon. "You want some help?" I shouted. She shook her head and waved me away.

Upstairs I laid my snack out carefully on my desk and tossed Dandy his bone. I will eat two cookies, drink the milk, and then call Nicky, I told myself. I ate three cookies, drank the milk, and did nothing. I ate two more cookies. I went into the bathroom for a glass of water. The phone rang.

"I'll get it!" I yelled.

It was Cara. "Did you call yet?" she asked.

"No, I'm having a snack first. Building up my strength. But I will. Just give me a couple more minutes."

I hung up and immediately left the room. Finding myself back in the hall for no good reason, I returned to the bathroom, brushed my teeth and combed my hair. Then I forced myself into Mom's room again, and took out the phone book. I found the number, took a deep breath, considered passing out, and dialed.

"Hello."

"Nicky?"

"Yes." His voice seemed guarded. Who was he expecting?

"It's me, Heather Connelly. I noticed you weren't in school, and I was worried." "Worried" sounded too personal, I decided, too pushy. *"Concerned,"* I added quickly.

"Oh. Well. Yeah."

Was that all he was going to say? What was I supposed to do next? All I could think of was Cara's advice: If at first you don't succeed, eat something.

"Are you all right?" I ventured at last, after a panicked pause.

I heard a deep sigh on the other end of the line. "Yeah, I'm fine. We had kind of an emergency here, but it's okay now. I'll be back in school Monday."

"Anything serious?"

"No. Not really."

He was obviously not going to explain, which left me to get out of the conversation as gracefully as I could.

"You missed a lot of geometry," I said on a sudden inspiration. "If you'd like to come over sometime this weekend, I could help you catch up."

Finally, the hint of a chuckle rippled in my ear.

"I'd like that," he said. "It has a familiar ring to it."

"How about tomorrow?"

"I'll try."

"Great."

"Heather?"

"Yes?"

"I may not make it. Things come up . . . sometimes."

"That's okay. Just let me know one way or the other."

"Thanks. I'll call you. Bye."

I don't know why I felt so good when I hung up, but I did. Tremendous progress had not been made, but I picked Dandy up and hugged him close, tickling my face against his soft, floppy ear. Close. Close is nice, I said to myself. Then I laughed, because it sounded kind of silly.

Dinner looked, smelled, and tasted heavenly. There was even a new strawflower centerpiece on the table.

"All this for just the two of us?" I exclaimed, then was sorry I'd said it. Mom's face fell.

"It's your favorite," she said quietly.

"I know. I love it. I just meant . . ."

"There'll be plenty for sandwiches next week."

"That's terrific." I meant it, but somehow my enthusiasm was too little, too late. We ate quietly for a while, then I decided to break the silence with the news about Nicky.

"Remember the guy I told you about, Mom? Nicky Simpson, in my geometry class? He may come over this weekend to work on some assignments he missed. That's okay, isn't it?"

"Of course. Anytime."

We smiled at each other across the centerpiece, anxious, polite smiles. I expected her to ask questions, lots of them—such as what was he like and where did he live and how did we meet and how come he never showed up the last time—all the stuff mothers are supposed to be curious about. But she never did.

9

Nicky arrived after lunch on Sunday. He emerged from his car in a pale blue sweater and jeans, looking as if he'd polished himself from head to toe for the occasion. I'd been out in the yard taking advantage of the break in the weather to try to teach Dandy to heel. My face stung with the cold, and when we went inside and I pulled off my scarf and hat, I could hear the electricity crackle and feel my hair standing out on end. Fortunately, Nicky was facing away from me and toward the kitchen door.

"Warm cinnamon and apples," he was saying with reverence in his voice. It gave me time to check the hall mirror and pat my hair into a semblance of order. The red cheeks and nose I could do nothing about.

"Yes, Mom's baking," I began just as Mom emerged from the kitchen, the sweet aroma wafting through the swinging door along with her. I ducked back into the living room just in time for introductions.

"Mom, this is Nicky Simpson. Nicky, my mom."

Mom beamed up at Nicky—she was about half his size—and immediately offered him lunch.

"No, thank you. I've eaten lunch," Nicky said, with a slight emphasis on "lunch," as opposed to, I guessed, "dessert."

Mom picked up the signal, too. "Then how about a piece of pie?" she said. "Dutch apple, fresh out of the oven."

"Cooking is Mom's hobby," I explained. "By all rights I should weigh three hundred pounds. I'm just lucky she doesn't have time to cook as much as she'd like to."

Nicky kind of shuffled around shyly for a second or two, then admitted he could probably find room for Dutch apple pie fresh out of the oven.

"I thought so," Mom said, spinning on her heel to lead the way into her warm and fragrant kitchen.

The thought occurred to me that Nicky's phone call that morning announcing his intended arrival and Mom's disappearance into the kitchen shortly thereafter were not coincidentally related. If there's one thing Mom knows how to do, it's to cook her way into a person's heart. She's been known to bake pies by the half dozen in her double oven, donating two or three to charity bake sales while Eddie and I, Daddy and Uncle Will—alone or in chorus—protested that charity began at home. Now she was encouraging Nicky to munch his way slice by slice through an entire pie, much to his amusement—and gratification.

"A growing boy," Mom observed with a happy sigh as Nicky topped off his fourth slice with a third glass of milk.

"A boy who's never had homemade pie fresh from the oven," Nicky admitted.

Mom's eyes widened. "Never?" she echoed.

"No, ma'am. My stepmother works, and even if she didn't, she's not much of a cook."

Stepmother? I thought. Mom and her apple pie now knew more about Nicky after twenty minutes than anyone at Hanover High had learned in four months.

"Then you'll take one pie home with you," Mom said.

"Oh, I couldn't do that."

"Why not?"

Nicky glanced from Mom to me. I shrugged. I couldn't see why not either.

"Okay," he said finally, his face alight with more smile than he'd ever shown at school. "Thank you. I'd love to."

A pitiful bark from the backyard broke into our warm cinnamon-and-apple lethargy and set us all into action.

"Poor Dandy hates being outside alone," I explained, opening the back door and letting the furry tan streak zip inside. "He thinks he's people, and if no other people are out there, he doesn't understand why he should be."

"I can see his point," Nicky said, laughing. Dandy was eagerly sniffing up one of Nicky's legs, across the knees and down the other. He sneezed, shook his head, ears flapping, and started all over again.

"Can I pick him up?" Nicky asked.

"You've never had a dog, either?" I asked.

"Uh-uh."

"Go on. Pick him up, put him down, toss him a bone. He appreciates any kind of attention you can spare," I said, helping Mom stack dishes and glasses in the sink.

"You go do your studying," she said, giving me a gentle shove as she turned on the water.

"Okay. Thanks for the pie."

"Yes, thank you, Mrs. Connelly," Nicky put in, standing up with Dandy in his arms. "It was delicious."

"My pleasure," Mom assured him.

"Go on and take Dandy into the living room," I said. "I'll go upstairs and get my books."

I had to take a minute in my room for deep breathing and pulling myself together. Everything was going so well, it was kind of overwhelming. I'd been so nervous about Nicky coming, so sure it would be an awkward day with nothing to talk about but geometry, and long silences in between formulas, I'd actually invited Cara to join us. "Not on your life!" she'd replied. "But call me the minute he leaves. I'll be waiting with my hand on the receiver."

I gave my hair a quick going over, grabbed my books, and was on my way to the door when Daddy's photograph caught my eye. How sad that he and Nicky had just missed each other! No, no crying, I told myself. Absolutely not. If Mom can be brave and fill up her life with a new job and apple pie, then so can I.

When I got downstairs, Nicky was on his back on the living room rug and Dandy was sprawled across his chest, licking the memory of pie crumbs off his face. I settled on the rug beside them, my back propped against the sofa. Immediately, Dandy pounced into my lap and tried to clean my face as well.

"Sit," I told him, setting him firmly on the floor in front of me.

Dandy smiled his puppy smile and stood there defiantly.

"I'm trying to train him," I explained to Nicky, "but it may be too late. He's already spoiled rotten."

"He's terrific," Nicky said.

"Sit!" I instructed Dandy.

He trotted over next to Nicky and sat down.

"I don't believe it," I groaned.

"You didn't say *where*," Nicky pointed out. "What else can't he do?"

"Lie down!" I commanded.

Dandy shot across the room, pulled his raggedy rawhide bone out from behind the easy chair, and set it down proudly next to Nicky's sneakered foot.

"Heel! Beg! Shake hands! Come! Stay! Roll over!" I cried in vain while Dandy blithely ignored me and Nicky almost got sick laughing.

Eventually we got our geometry done, in spite of Dandy's trotting across our books and papers. There was no awkwardness at all, not even during the silences. It was as if we'd always been there together on my living-room floor, talking parallelograms and puppies.

When Nicky finally left, foil-wrapped Dutch apple pie balanced carefully on top of his books, his promise to return seemed to fill up the emptiness that had lingered so long in our house. I passed through the kitchen on my way to letting Dandy out and heard Mom humming as she wiped the counters clean.

Is that what we'd always need? I wondered. A third person to hold us together?

10

"Rumor has it," Cara said, sneaking up behind me at my locker and scaring me half to death, "that you and Nicky Simpson have a date Friday night."

I whirled around to face her evil grin. "You found out already?" I gasped. "How?"

"I haff my vays," she intoned huskily. "But why wasn't I the third to know?"

"He caught me outside English class. You and I don't have English together or anything after that."

"True. Well, I guess you're forgiven. So what's it going to be? Movies? Dinner? Dancing? A night on the town, as they say?"

"Bowling."

"Bowling?"

"He likes to bowl."

"But you don't know how to bowl. Do you?"

"No," I admitted, "but believe you me, I intend to learn."

We zipped on our layers of protection against the snow and ice and ventured outside. With my first step I nearly slid down the sidewalk and had to grab hold of Cara's arm for support.

"Cara, I am scared," I said, righting myself on the ice and shifting my books back into place.

"Don't worry. You're well padded. You won't break."

"Not about falling! I've never been out with a guy who drives."

"As long as he keeps driving," Cara pointed out, "you've got nothing to worry about. The problem's when they *stop*."

Nicky picked me up promptly at eight that Friday night and took my mittened hand as we negotiated the fresh snow piling up on our front porch steps. Patches and lumps of ice lay underneath, making the descent all the more treacherous.

"I'm afraid I don't do a very good job shoveling," I said. "It's tough not having a man around the house anymore."

"Is that a hint?" Nicky asked.

"Oh, no, not at all. I'm just apologizing in advance in case you fall and break your neck."

"Good, because if it was a hint, I couldn't take you up on it. My stepmother has enough for me to do to last three lifetimes, and she's *got* a man around the house."

I caught a glimpse of Nicky's face as he opened the car door for me and the interior light went on. He looked grim, but he didn't elaborate on his stepmother's demands. The rusty hinges of the car door shrieked in protest as he swung it shut.

"Do you have any brothers or sisters?" I asked when he'd settled in behind the steering wheel. For a moment we fumbled in silence for matching ends to our seat belts.

"No," he responded at last. "Well, yes, kind of. My stepmother has two preschoolers."

I waited, but again no more information was forthcoming. I pressed on. "Boys or girls?"

"One of each. Brad's two; Kim's almost four."

He started the car and gave his attention to maneuvering the slick streets. Apparently Dandy and the apple pie had only postponed the awkwardness of our getting to know each other.

"My brother moved to Oregon last June, after graduation," I said.

"That's when we moved here. June twenty-ninth."

"June must be National Moving Month," I observed, immediately aware that I was starting to babble nonsense. "School's out, I guess that's why. And you have the whole summer to get used to it. Where did you move from?" I asked finally, desperate to turn the conversation around even though I already knew the answer to my question.

"Kansas City."

"Did you like it there?"

"Not bad."

"You miss your friends?"

"Not really."

I sighed and gave up trying. This was a new Nicky, not the shy one, not the relaxed, playful one. This one was sullen and tight-lipped. How many more were there? It was a relief to get to the bowling alley and busy ourselves with finding balls and changing shoes.

"Know how to bowl?" Nicky asked.

"You roll the ball and knock down the pins," I answered airily. "How hard can it be?"

Waving him aside, I heaved the ball to my hip and then to my chest, stumbled forward three or four steps, and let 'er rip. The ball crashed to the floor, alarming bowlers to either side of me, then rumbled its way into the gutter.

For the first time that evening, Nicky laughed. I didn't mind.

"Allow me," he said, and proceeded to let me in on several dozen of the finer points of bowling technique.

Lost in the intricacies of hand and foot positions, knee bending, wrist action, floor markings, and seven-ten splits, Nicky apparently forgot whatever was going on at home that had made him unhappy. For all its noise, the bowling alley did have a soothing rhythm to it: click, rumble, crash, rumble, click—and lots of laughter. My score rose game by game from 29 to 87. Teacher and pupil were both very pleased, and the ride home was alive with plans for my weekly training sessions and brilliant career on the bowling-for-bucks circuit.

But as we pulled into our driveway and rolled to a stop, the talk turned serious.

"I guess it's time I explained myself," Nicky began. "If we're going to be seeing each other—" He stopped short and peered at me across the darkened car. "We are going to be seeing each other, aren't we?"

"I hope so," I said.

"Well, then, here goes. When school started this year, I didn't want to make any friends. I'd pretty much decided never to care about anybody ever again."

"Why on earth not?"

Nicky took a deep breath and exhaled a stream of steamy air. "When my dad got promoted and we moved down here, he started working twice as hard, twice as long. We used to be really close, but not anymore. He's either at the plant or worrying that he should be. That's

where he met Eve. They got married three weeks after
their first date, just went off one weekend and came
back married. And boom, there I was with these two
little brats in my house and a slave-driving stepmother.
By the time school started, I'd decided the fewer people
I let into my life, the better off I'd be. Only I guess
I'm not the big, tough loner I thought I was. I knew you
were . . . um . . . interested, and I was, too."

I blushed, remembering all the dumb things I'd done
to get his attention, the little-girl games I'd been playing while he was suffering grown-up pain. All that time
I'd wanted him to notice me, and now I felt even
dumber knowing he had.

"That time I couldn't help you with your math," he
went on, "I had to stay home with the kids. Same reason
I missed nearly a week of school. Their baby-sitter was
sick and Eve didn't want to take off from work. Stuff
like that comes up all the time. I thought you'd better
know."

"I'm glad you told me," I said quietly.

"Yeah. I'm glad I did, too."

He was still looking straight ahead, his arms resting
on top of the steering wheel, his left hand stroking little
zigzags and squiggles in the steam condensing on the
windshield. It occurred to me that he'd never mentioned his real mother, or how long he and his dad had
been alone before Eve. The collar of his navy peacoat
was flipped up on the side closest to me. It made him
look like he needed caring for.

As long as he keeps driving . . . I heard Cara say. *The
problem's when they stop.*

Little did she know.

All of a sudden I realized *I* was the one thinking
about kissing. I really wanted to kiss Nicky just then,

and that struck me as odd, interesting but odd. Before—
ever since spin the bottle in fifth grade and the parties
that suddenly went dark in junior high—I'd just wanted
to kiss: to see what it was like, to be doing what everybody else was doing, to have something exciting to report to Cara. This was the first time ever that I wanted
to kiss somebody in particular. Nicky. I wished I could
think of some way to make it happen.

I shifted in my seat and Nicky finally looked my way.
Then he moved his hand from the steering wheel to
my shoulder and, easy as that, my wish came true.

11

"Woman talk, that's what I need," Liz Dale announced over the phone the next morning. "A female fix. I've been matching wits all week with condescending, patronizing, pigheaded men at the office. How about you and your mom and Cara and me going out to lunch today?"

Liz is a very successful advertising account executive, and I pity any man foolish enough to condescend in her presence.

"Sure," I said. "We'd love to. It's either that or clean house."

"Knowing your mom, she's already cleaned next week's dirt in advance. We'll pick you up in forty-five minutes. The Greenery at the mall okay? Cara started Diet Eight Hundred last night at dinner—immediately after the pecan pie—so it has to be a salad bar."

"Sounds great. See you in forty-five minutes."

"It's either what or clean house?" Mom wanted to know. She was in the living room furiously working a crochet hook down the long edge of an afghan she was making for Eddie and Marie. Woolen folds in soft shades of green covered her from lap to floor.

"How could you hear what I was saying through two rooms and a closed door?" I asked.

"Mothers are born with good hearing. House cleaning or what?"

"Or we go out to lunch with Cara and Liz at the Greenery. How about it? You want to?"

Mom lowered the afghan and pursed her lips thoughtfully. "I don't know," she said.

"Come on, Mom. We haven't been out together since . . . for a long time."

"I'd better not. I have to get this afghan finished and in the mail by Monday. But you go ahead. I'll take a rain check."

"Oh, Mom, Liz wants us both to come," I protested. But Mom shook her head. "You go on," she said, and set her hook and yarn to flying again.

Forty-five minutes later I was climbing into the back seat of the Dale Chevette, alone.

"Mom sends her regrets," I announced with a cheerfulness I was no longer feeling. "She's up to her elbows in an afghan she's trying to get to Oregon in time for Eddie's birthday."

"Oh, that's too bad," Liz said. "I've hardly seen your mother since your father died."

"Neither have I," I said, struggling to keep my tone light. "She's the new dispatcher for the Home Meals program at the hospital. She has to arrange for drivers to take hot lunches all over town. Sometimes she has to drive a route or two herself when the volunteers don't show up. She has all kinds of meetings to go to at night. Plus her bridge game. She's really busy."

"That's good. Boy, do I ever admire volunteer workers. I mean, I get up and out in the morning because we wouldn't eat if I didn't. I'd really rather be tanning myself on the Riviera, but hunger is very motivating. For volunteer work, though, you have to . . . *volunteer!*"

"Brilliant," Cara muttered from the seat in front of mine. It occurred to me that this was the first word she'd spoken since I'd gotten into the car.

"Hello, Cara," I said.

"Hello," she answered, without turning around.

"Cara is weird this morning," Liz explained. "She's promised to tell us both at once what's bothering her. She says it's not a tale worth telling twice."

"So what is it?" I asked.

"Food first," Cara said.

At the Greenery, Liz and I exchanged looks of curiosity as we stood in line for the salad bar and filled our plates. Lagging behind, Cara kept mum.

"It's hard," Liz pointed out when we'd all convened at our table, "to pile seven thousand calories' worth of salad onto one small plate, but I believe Cara's done it." Her beautiful blue eyes widened with mock amazement.

"I've come to a decision," Cara said, carefully setting down her vegetable mountain before taking her seat.

"Not another bizarre diet," her mother moaned. "I can't take any more. Grapefruit, alfalfa sprouts, an entire week of hard-boiled eggs. I've had enough! If I've told you once, I've told you a million times, you'll slim down at the end of your teens just like I did. . . ."

"You slimmed down at the end of your teens because you had me to take care of and nobody to take care of you," Cara snapped. "But no, it's not another diet. Not exactly. What I've decided is this: Life is too short not to eat everything you can get your hands on."

Liz gasped and I choked on my mouthful of greens.

"And what," Liz said, "brought you to that conclusion?"

"My date last night. I was nearly raped. Who knows? I could have been murdered. That's when I decided life's too short to deny myself anything. 'Eating well is the best revenge.' Didn't somebody once say that?"

"I believe the expression is 'Living well is the best revenge,' " Liz said.

"Eating well, living well—it's the same thing, isn't it?"

"If you say so," Liz conceded. "But what revenge are you trying to get? What murder? What rape?"

"All in good time," Cara said, taking a sip of water.

Liz rolled her eyes in exasperation, but we both knew Cara well enough to see she was beginning to enjoy her own bad mood.

"How was your date with Nicky?" Cara asked me, pretending sudden interest.

"Wonderful," I said.

"Care to elaborate?"

"Nope."

"Cara . . ." Liz began, impatience rising in her voice.

"Okay, okay," Cara said. "Brace yourselves." She gave us a moment to do so, then began. "As you know, I was out with Dennis Gould last night, straight-A student, Merit Scholarship finalist, darling of teachers everywhere, and part-time sex maniac."

"What?" Liz and I chorused.

"In the basement of the Gould household," Cara went on, "on a brown tweed sofa across from the complete works of Shakespeare bound in Moroccan leather and stereo components fit for the gods, occurred a wrestling match I do not wish to describe in gory detail."

Liz grabbed her glass and took a gulp of water, but the snicker she was trying to drown burst out anyway.

"Lost control of his hormones, did he?" she gasped through a short fit of coughing.

"What kind of a mother makes excuses for the *boy*?" Cara exclaimed.

"Oh, keep your voice down," Liz suggested, still chuckling.

"I don't care who hears it," Cara continued in a rasping whisper, a smile twitching at the corners of her mouth in spite of her outrage. "He was crazy. I mean, it had nothing to do with affection—or even *desire*. It was like he was in a competition of some kind, like he had to prove something to somebody."

"Maybe he did," Liz said, finally managing a straight face.

"Well, tough," Cara rasped on. "Nobody, and I mean nobody, uses one inch of this too, too solid flesh here to prove anything to anybody without my permission."

"So what did you do?" Liz managed to ask, her eyes growing moist again with suppressed laughter.

"First I asked him to stop and then I ordered him to stop and then I warned him he had damn well better stop and then I ripped off his glasses and hurled them across the room. The crash finally got his attention."

"Oh, no!" Liz cried. "Does this mean we have to pay for new glasses?"

"I thought of that," Cara told her, "and I suppose we will. Just as soon as he tells his parents how those got broken and they send us a bill. 'Dear Ms. Dale: The following damages occurred while our son was attempting to molest your daughter. Please pay last amount in column.' "

Liz and I burst into laughter so loud, the line at the salad bar stopped and all heads turned toward us as one. It took Cara only a second or two to join us.

"Oh, poor Dennis," Liz wheezed.

"Why do you keep worrying about *him*?" Cara asked,

using a napkin to catch the tears running down her
cheeks. "You're *my* mother, remember?"

"Who could forget? And I have to worry about him
because there's no sense worrying about you."

"It is dreadful," Cara said, turning her attention to
me, "to have a mother who trusts you completely. It's as
if she's sure you couldn't get into trouble even if you
tried. What an insult."

"Oh, you can get into it," Liz said, smiling affection-
ately at Cara. "What I'm so sure of is that you'll always
get back out. Right, Heather?"

"Right," I said.

But Cara and Liz were kind of glowing across the
table at each other and neither heard me.

I wished my mom had come.

12

As winter deepened, Mom seemed to wrap herself ever more tightly in a blanket of solitude thick as Eddie's afghan. She was there in the house with me, still cooking and cleaning up a storm when she wasn't rushing off to work or signing up for night classes, and yet she wasn't there at all, at least not so that I could really reach her.

Nicky seemed able to draw her out some, but what with his obligations at home and his new part-time job busing tables at the China Dragon, his visits were few and far between.

He and I did manage to attend the Sweetheart Ball in February. We double-dated with Cara and a gorgeous hunk of varsity letterman named K. A. McKuen ("The Human Typhoon"). K.A. spoke two languages fluently: Basketball Statistic and Football Statistic. His ability to recite personal and team data coast to coast and throughout history was not what appealed to Cara, however; he was also a terrific dancer. I learned a lot about sports that night, and a little more about Nicky.

Music seemed to blast the gym doors open as we

arrived. Close-packed bodies were already gyrating around the giant spotlighted heart in the center of the floor. No sooner had Cara hung up her coat than K.A. whisked her into the crowd and set all four of his long limbs to pulsating in time to the hard-rock beat. Jaw clenched, brow furrowed in concentration, he seemed engaged in private combat with the music—and determined to win. Cara waved my way, then threw her head back and laughed in delight as K.A. spun, wriggled, and writhed in circles around her.

Meanwhile, Nicky had wandered off in the direction of the refreshment table. Tearing myself away from K.A.'s performance, I trailed him to a glass punch bowl filled with potato chips. Nicky looked troubled. He'd been quiet in the car, but I'd assumed K.A.'s running sportscast had caused that.

"Want a Coke?" he asked. "Some chips?"

"No, thanks," I said.

He grabbed a handful of chips and began munching. We watched dancers dance. The song ended. Nicky reached for a Coke. We watched dancers rest, then dance again. I began to wonder if Nicky were twins: one open, warm, and easy to get along with, the other silent, brooding, and secretive. If so, the wrong twin had come to this dance.

The music began again. Nicky polished off his drink and stretched across the table toward a basket brimming with pretzel sticks.

"If you're hungry," I told him, "we could go get a hamburger or something."

"I'm not hungry," he said quickly.

Our eyes traced parallel paths to the pretzels now clutched in his fist. When I looked up again, he was blushing.

"Nicky," I said, "do you know how to dance?"

"Nope."

"Why didn't you *say* something?"

His shoulders rose to his ears in an embarrassed shrug.

"Were you planning to eat everything on this table?"

He grinned sheepishly.

"And then what?" I went on. "Get sick and go home?"

"I hadn't thought that far ahead," he admitted, "but thanks for the idea."

It was lucky he started to laugh just then, because I was having a lot of trouble holding back my giggles. I took his hand, shook out the pretzel sticks, and led him to a corner of the gym far from the spotlight's glare.

"Left, together, right, together, step, together, step," we began.

The evening, which ended with a series of slow dances under fading lights, brought us closer together in more ways than one.

In return for the dancing lessons, Nicky volunteered to teach me how to drive. The drivers' ed. class at school was so huge, we were each lucky if we got four hours' practice in a school car. The end of our four hours saw us able to maneuver the school parking lot, but not much else.

Nicky gave me a gold heart pendant for my sixteenth birthday in March, and we broached the driving subject with Mom as she was oohing and aahing over my gift. She agreed that Nicky was a born teacher—my bowling average had already risen to 125! And, of course, she was terribly busy.

My lessons were scheduled for Saturdays and Sundays at dawn, the one part of Nicky's day no one else had laid claim to. I am not, by nature, a morning person. Watching me back a car out of our long driveway while still immersed in my personal fog would have been enough to send a less patient teacher screaming into the sunrise. When you consider that it was *his* car I was endangering—his hard-earned car now maintained through hours and hours of dumping oriental garbage—Nicky practically qualified for sainthood.

I got my license at the end of April, on the first try. That meant I owed Nicky dinner out and a movie. He'd bet I could do it the first time out, and I'd bet against myself. What did I know? I'd never been awake to watch myself drive.

"Told you, *told you* you were ready," Nicky crowed, as if passing the test had been his triumph instead of mine. "Huh? Huh? Didn't I tell you? Dinner for two at the China Dragon, I think."

"Chinese food?" I said. "On your night off? Don't you get enough of that five nights a week?"

"I want the guys at work to see you pick up the tab."

"Gonna milk this thing for all it's worth, aren't you?" I observed dryly. "You taught me how to drive, Simpson, not how to *fly*."

I paid my fee, got my picture taken, and we left the State Office Building arm in arm.

"And after dinner," Nicky continued, "I wouldn't mind seeing *E.T.* again."

"For the third time? You just enjoy watching me cry at the end, don't you?" When E.T. touches Elliot's forehead just before leaving Earth for good and tells Elliot he'll always be there, in Elliot's mind, it makes me think of Daddy and how he exists only in my memory now, and pretty near breaks my heart."

"No, I don't enjoy watching you cry," Nicky said, suddenly serious. "I just like the movie. If you'd rather not go . . ."

"No, that's okay. I like it, too. How about next Friday?"

"Uh-uh, it's Kim's birthday. We'll probably have to celebrate at McDonald's, and they'll expect me to be there. And Saturday, I have to work. Friday after that?"

"It's a date. You want flowers?"

"Yeah," Nicky said, laughing, "a bouquet of dandelions."

The night of the lost-bet dinner, Nicky was to pick me up at six. I'd offered to pick him up, new driver's license and all, but he'd declined. I'd never once in the three months we'd been dating been to his house. He didn't seem overly anxious to have me meet his father and stepmother.

At twenty till six I was frantically blowing my hair dry for the second time, having dashed back under the shower in despair after the first attempt. I was considering shaving my head when I heard Mom yelling from her room that I had a phone call.

"What? What?" I cried impatiently, shutting off the dryer to make sure I'd heard right.

"Nicky's on the phone."

I made a last swipe at the stubborn cowlick behind my left ear and tossed my brush onto the dresser.

"Be right there," I said. On impulse I grabbed the hairspray and squirted the demon cowlick flat.

"What did you do to your hair?" Mom asked as our paths crossed in her doorway.

"I don't care to discuss it," I said, and snatched up the receiver.

"Date's off," Nicky announced, without so much as a hello. "Brad and Kim are down with chicken pox, my dad and Eve have some kind of company dinner to go

to, their regular sitter is out of town, and they don't
want to leave sick kids with a stranger."

"But we've had this date planned for two weeks. We
have reservations."

"Don't you think I know that?" Nicky snapped. "We'll
just have to do it another time. They can't cancel."

"Oh, wow, Nicky, and I had this nice wilted dandelion for you and everything. I found/it last Tuesday.
First dandelion of the season."

Nicky was not amused. "Terrific," he muttered, as if
missing out on a wilted dandelion were just one more in
a long parade of disappointments.

"Hey, I could bring it by," I said, suddenly inspired.
"I could get Chinese carry-out and bring it all by. I
don't mind baby-sitting."

"Well, gee, I don't know . . ."

"Go ask your folks," I insisted. "Go ahead. I'll ask my
mom."

Two minutes later we were both back on the phone.

"They said it's okay with them if it's okay with your
mom," Nicky said.

"My mom said it's okay with her if it's okay with
them."

"Then I guess it's okay," Nicky concluded, beginning
to warm up to the idea. "Have you had chicken pox?"

"Sure. See you soon."

I phoned our order in to the China Dragon, stuck a
barrette over my problem hair, grabbed the wilted dandelion, and was on my way.

Nicky's house was not in a neighborhood I fre-
quented. It was a new development of nearly identical
ranch-style houses behind the typewriter plant where
his parents worked. Where my block had giant maples
and pin oaks, his was lined with newly planted saplings.

Runoff from the spring rains had worn crisscrossed miniature riverbeds through the packed mud of several lots that had yet to be seeded for grass. Nicky's was one of these.

I felt nervous and more than a little silly ringing the bell with my arms full of Chinese food. I was toying with the idea of leaving the order and bowing my way back to my car when Mrs. Simpson opened the door.

I don't know what I was expecting—a giantess, maybe, with moles on her chin and wielding a club—but she wasn't it. Olive-skinned and gaunt, she was neither grotesque nor pretty. What she was was *plain*, even in her flowery pink dress. She seemed too old to be the mother of preschoolers, but as she led me into the house and introduced me to Mr. Simpson—potbellied, with Nicky's dark, straight hair, brown eyes, and shy smile— I studied her more closely and realized she wasn't as old as she seemed at first glance. She probably hadn't slept much, what with two sick kids, and if that weren't enough to spoil her appearance, she was also about twice as nervous as I was.

"I'm sorry things don't look any better," she told me, twitching the belt of her dress one minute and the slip-cover over the sofa the next. "What with working and all, we really haven't had much of a chance to fix the place up."

"Looks fine to me," I lied, handing Nicky the packages of food. Grateful for something to do and someplace to go, he quickly disappeared into the kitchen while the Simpsons and I looked each other over and continued our awkward attempts at conversation. Actually, Mrs. Simpson and I did most of the talking. Mr. Simpson mainly wore his uncomfortable smile and nodded agreement to whatever was said.

The tension snapped abruptly when one of the children cried "Mommy!" from a bedroom at the end of the hall.

"If we don't leave now, we'll never get out," Mr. Simpson told his wife.

"Ma-ahmmmy!" the little voice wailed again. "My throat hurts me."

"Me too," a second voice chimed in.

Mrs. Simpson's gaze wavered between the hallway and her husband. She hesitated a moment, then called toward the kitchen: "Handle it, will you, Nicky? Please?"

Mr. Simpson nodded farewell and ushered her out the door.

13

At last Nicky emerged from the kitchen. "Time to meet the brats," he said, taking my hand and leading me down the hall.

Kim and Brad, bleary-eyed and flushed with fever and pox, lay in twin beds on opposite sides of a sparsely furnished room. A couple of braided rugs dotted the wood floor and the bare walls were painted blue. The children were so full of their own misery, they eyed me without much curiosity and never even asked who I was. I watched while Nicky gave them each baby aspirin and drinks of water, and brushed their damp hair off their faces gently with his free hand.

Back in the kitchen, the dandelion sat in a paper cup in the center of the wooden table, drooping pitifully, but surrounded by an inviting array of plates, table settings, and bowls of egg rolls, rice, moo goo gai pan, and cashew chicken.

"Hey, I was supposed to be treating you tonight," I said. "I should have done all this."

Nicky shrugged off my objection and pulled back a chair for me. We sat across from each other and got through the first shy moments of being alone in a house together—his house, at that—by getting the food passed, served, tasted, and commented on.

"I guess you can see why I haven't invited you here before," Nicky said after we'd finally run out of ways to discuss our meal.

"No, I can't," I told him.

"Well, compared to your house, this isn't much."

"Were we in a contest?" I asked.

Nicky smiled. "I guess not. It's just that—well, the move here was a big break for my dad, but mortgages these days . . ."

"I know all about mortgages. My father explained it to me when he took out mortgage insurance on our house. I guess—" I had to stop for a moment, caught off guard by my own train of thought. "I guess he suspected he wouldn't be around to meet the payments," I went on. "Mom has always hated talking about things like wills and insurance policies, so he told me everything he thought we both needed to know. In case . . . things turned out the way they did. Actually, our lawyer took care of everything. But I do know our interest rate is probably half of yours."

"To be perfectly honest," Nicky admitted, "I haven't the slightest idea what ours is, except that it's high. Are you going to be an accountant like your father was?"

"Maybe. Or a stockbroker. There's a bit of the gambler in me."

"I know. That's how I got this dinner. I wouldn't make a career out of it, though, if I were you."

Laughing, he checked all our bowls for leftovers. I refused his offer of third helpings, so he mounded everything that remained onto his own plate and dug in.

"Actually," I informed him, "this was an off night in a long and successful career. Every night for years, Daddy and I played this game where we'd read the stock reports and pretend to choose stocks to buy and sell."

"You can read the stock reports? All those columns of weird numbers?"

"Sure. I've made many a fortune in my day. On paper, that is."

"Great! A girlfriend who'll make me rich!"

"I've lost a couple of fortunes, too."

"Uh-oh."

"How about you? What do you want to be?"

Nicky put down his fork and glanced across at me shyly.

"Promise you won't laugh?" he asked.

"Of course I won't."

"I want to be a writer, a novelist. I want to write books."

"*Really?*"

"Yeah. I've never told that to anyone before."

"Why not? I think it's wonderful. Have you—" I never got to finish my question. Nicky had already leaped to his feet and was gathering up bowls and silverware.

"Hey!" he said. "We can still catch part of the *Star Trek* rerun on TV. You want to?"

"You go on," I told him. "Let me clean up."

"Don't you like *Star Trek?*"

"I love it, especially Mr. Spock. Call me when he comes on. This dinner was supposed to be my treat, so let me *treat.*"

Feeling very domestic, I scraped the dishes, found the detergent, and plunged my hands into a sinkful of warm bubbles while Nicky settled himself into a large reclining chair in front of the TV. Neither of us saw much of Mr. Spock, though, because Kim and Brad required several more visits and reassurances before falling asleep.

A truly corny western had begun by the time I finally emerged from the kitchen, smoothing on a dab of Mrs. Simpson's hand lotion. Nicky was back in the recliner and motioned me to join him. Somehow I wedged myself in. After flipping up the footrest, he wriggled himself into position for a long, Chinese-flavored kiss. I snuggled down against his shoulder.

"What were you thinking," I said, feeling cozy and just a little giddy, "all those times when I was trying to get you to notice me?"

"Scared," he said. "Shy. Silly. Mad at myself."

"Mad at yourself? Why?"

"For being scared, shy, and silly. That time you asked me if I was having trouble with the math assignment . . ."

"Oh, God, don't remind me."

"I couldn't believe I said no. For the rest of the day I kept thinking of all the clever, witty things I *should* have said."

"Like what?"

"Like *yes*. If I'd only said yes, think of all the trouble I would have saved myself. Like going to the Snow Ball for nothing."

"Remember the Homecoming Dance—when I just came up and stood next to you? Did you realize . . ."

"Yes, and I panicked. I just panicked and went home."

"I was devastated," I said, laughing. "If only I'd known then what I do now—that you couldn't ask me to dance because you didn't know how."

"If only I'd had the guts to try. That's what you've done for me, Heather. You've given me guts."

"Guts! That has such a romantic ring to it. Is that

all?" I asked, tilting my head back to enjoy the closeness of those wonderful brown eyes. They loomed above me for a moment, then closed as we kissed again, shifting to press ourselves even more closely together.

"You know what, Nicky?" I said on the spur of the moment. "I think I love you."

"*What?*"

I looked up to find his face blanched with surprise.

"Don't get hysterical," I said. "This doesn't mean you have to marry me or anything. It's just that—well, I used to worry about love a lot, that something was wrong with me because I'd never felt that way about a boy. And just now I suddenly realized I do feel that way about you. It kind of sneaked up on me. I thought you might like to know. No big deal."

"Bigger deal than you think."

"What do you mean?"

"Well, I think I love you, too."

We both sighed and giggled at our sighing, then held each other quietly for a long time. Someday, I thought dreamily, we'll make love, Nicky and I, when we're ready, and it won't be to prove anything to anybody, and it won't be because we have nothing to say to each other. "Making love" is exactly what it will be.

A wail from the back bedroom pierced our cocoon. Nicky worked his way out of the chair and went to see what the problem was. I switched off the TV, sending horses, men, and cattle into a permanent cloud of gray dust.

"You're going to make somebody a terrific mother," I told Nicky when he came back into the living room. I'd meant it to be funny, but his face twitched into something closer to a grimace than a grin. Mothers, except for mine, were not his favorite topic.

"Want some coffee?" he asked abruptly.

"Sure." I followed him into the kitchen and got mugs off a rack while he fussed with the water and kettle.

"I could really go for one of your mother's Dutch apple pies right now," he said, piling a jar of instant coffee, a sugar bowl, a carton of milk, and spoons onto the table in front of me.

"I could call her," I offered. "One word from you and she'd probably bake one up and run it right over. She adores watching you eat."

"She's great," Nicky said.

I nodded; then, as he took his seat across from me, I ventured to say out loud what I'd only said to myself until then. "Nicky? Do you notice anything wrong with her? I mean, does she seem unhappy to you or anything like that?"

"Uh-uh. She seems fine. Why?"

"I don't know. It's just this feeling I have. Maybe it's just my imagination, but we seem to be drifting apart."

"Must be your imagination. She's there, isn't she? You want drifting apart, try *my* mother."

"You mean your stepmother? Eve?"

"No, I mean my real mother."

I'd picked up a spoon and now it clattered to the table. Nicky had never mentioned his real mother. I'd assumed she was dead.

"I lost her when I was eight," he began, then flipped his hair out of his eyes and started over. "No, that's not true. The truth is, she walked out."

"Walked out?"

"Just said she'd had enough one day, packed up, and left. Dad divorced her eventually. Once, when I asked about her, he told me some women were never meant to be wives and mothers, and she was one of them. I didn't understand what he meant by that. I still don't. I mean, she *was* a wife and mother, wasn't she? At any rate, I haven't seen or heard from her since."

"Oh, Nicky, that's awful. I'm so—"

But Nicky shook his head to stop me. The kettle began to whistle, and he quickly got up to grab it off the stove. Retrieving my spoon, I ladled coffee into our mugs and held them while he filled them with boiling water. He returned the kettle to the stove and sat down without looking at me.

"Sometimes I wish she'd died," he murmured.

"Oh, don't say that!"

"Not because I hate her. Because I can't stand knowing she's out there somewhere and I can't reach her. Not even to say hello. She's out there and she doesn't want to reach *me*."

He paused for a moment, slowly stirring sugar into his coffee. I longed to comfort him, but couldn't think of anything to say. What had happened was terrible; what words could make it better? Nicky put down his spoon and leaned back in his chair until he had it balanced on the two back legs. He was striking a pose that had to be far more nonchalant than he felt.

"No wonder I like *E.T.* so much, huh?" he said. "That ugly little space creature who's been left behind by his mother ship. He knows it's out there somewhere, but how can he possibly call it back? Only, he *does*. Boy, you think *you* get choked up at the ending."

He let his chair fall forward with a thud, catching himself with both hands on the edge of the table. Instinctively I reached out as if to block his fall, and he took my hands in his.

"Well, you're no ugly little space creature," I told him. "And I cry because it hurts when E.T. and Elliot have to say good-bye."

"At least they do get to say good-bye," Nicky pointed out. "If my mother had died . . ."

"I see what you mean. You'd know it was over."

"Right. And then I could get past that part, past the grief, and start remembering the good things. The way it is now, I'm always stuck right there, trying to say good-bye, but not really wanting to, not as long as there's still a little bit of hope. I can't close the wound, and I can't bear leaving it open."

"You have no idea where she is?"

"No. But she could find me easily enough, if she wanted to. Dad's changed jobs, but it's the same company."

We were still holding hands, mugs of cold coffee between us, when Mr. and Mrs. Simpson came home.

14

One balmy Saturday evening in May, a week and a half before the end of school, Nicky arrived at our house twenty minutes late for our planned trip to the bowling alley. With barely a nod toward Mom and a muttered greeting in my direction, he whisked me outside and into the car. I braced myself. After a fairly long absence, during which no one missed him, the gloomy Nicky was back. No sooner had he backed out of our driveway than he suddenly swerved the car onto a side street and braked it sharply at the curb.

"What in the world . . . ?" I gasped, grabbing the dashboard with both hands to keep my balance.

Nicky flipped off the ignition. "She threw me out of the house," he said.

"What?"

"You heard me. She wanted me to baby-sit tonight. Again. Never mind that we had plans. Never mind that we always have plans and all our plans go right down the toilet anytime she decides *they* have better plans. Well, this is it. I hate her guts and I hate her kids and that's all there is to it. I'm through."

I put my hand on his arm and tried to jolly him out of his mood. "Oh, come on, Nicky," I said. "This isn't like you. Talk sense. What's the problem? What happened tonight?"

Nicky shrugged my hand away. "I am talking sense," he snapped, "and you know what the problem is. You've been putting up with it, too."

"I haven't been putting up with anything."

"Well, I certainly have. Company banquets, company meetings, birthdays, weddings, funerals, chicken pox. You know what it was this time? *Absolutely nothing.* My father was still out at a meeting and she wanted to meet him afterward for a drink. I said no. Stay home and take care of your brats for a change. Some great marriage deal you got: a husband, a house, and a live-in servant. And the next thing I know, she's pushing me out the door, screaming and crying like a lunatic: 'I've had it with you! I'm sick of trying! It's not my fault I'm not your mother. Go on! Get out! Do whatever you want. Yes, this is *my* home now and you're not going to ruin it for me or *my* husband or *my* children. So, *go!*' "

"Oh, Nicky, she doesn't mean—"

"No, she's right. It's all hers now. So I've got to find what's mine. I'm going back to Kansas City and I'm going to find my mother."

"Don't you think you ought to discuss this with your dad?"

"Discuss what? Me and my wicked stepmother? She's *family* to him. He's crazy about those kids. Keeps promising to build them a tree house someday. Jeez, that stupid yard doesn't even have a tree. Well, great. Fine. Let 'em have each other, if that's what they want. I'll get what I want, too."

"What if you don't find her?" I asked softly.

Muscles twitched along Nicky's jaw. "I'll find her," he said.

"When do you plan to leave?" I asked, barely forcing the words past the pain swelling in my throat.

"The sooner, the better. Maybe tomorrow."

A light breeze wafted through the open car window, fragrant with spring. Somewhere out there, I thought sadly, is a perfectly beautiful evening. I turned my face into the breeze, letting it soothe me, giving Nicky time to think, I hoped. At least, giving myself time to think. The breeze dropped as suddenly as it had sprung up. Nicky began drumming his fingers against the seatback next to my ear.

"What about school?" I asked, turning toward him again.

His dark eyes flashed with annoyance. "What about it? There are other schools in the world."

"Sixteen-year-olds can't just walk in off the street and enroll in one."

"So I won't go to school. So what? The semester's almost over anyway. By next fall I'll figure something out."

"Like what? How to do your sophomore year over again? If you drop out now without taking your finals, you'll probably lose all your credits."

"So what?"

"Will you stop saying 'so what' and think this through?"

"I have thought it through. I'm leaving."

"Okay, so you're leaving. What difference will a couple of weeks make? You've stuck it out this long, why not stick it out till the end of the semester? That makes sense, doesn't it?"

And that would give me time to think and you time to

cool down and them time to shape up, I continued, but not out loud.

"I don't know," Nicky said slowly. "If I don't get out now . . ."

"You'll get out later. Nicky, you're going to need a job, and for that you're going to need an education. You know high school dropouts don't stand a chance. God, the way the economy is now, high school graduates hardly stand a chance."

"I'll be writing. I'll have a lot to write about."

"A book takes years. What'll you eat in the meantime?"

Nicky sucked in a long, deep breath and whistled it out slowly over his curled lower lip. "The rational math major strikes again," he said.

"Don't blame it on me," I told him. "Those are the facts whether you hear them from me or not, and you know it."

"Okay, okay, I'll stay till the end of the semester. I might as well work a few more nights. I'll need the money. But then I'm going. Are you coming with me?"

"No."

"I didn't think you would," he muttered.

"You don't have to say it like that. You're the one leaving me, not the other way around."

"That's true. I'm sorry. It's just . . . I have to." Eyes clouded with pain, he looked scared and lost and alone. I reached out, and we held each other for a while, as tightly as we could.

Later we drove to the bowling alley and bowled one game, out of habit, I guess. Nicky bowled a 126; I bowled a 133. Even he had to laugh a little at that.

I was home before ten and answered Mom's curious expression with half a lie. "Nicky had a really bad head-

ache," I told her, which conveniently accounted for his
bad mood when he'd picked me up, too. And he may
well have had a really bad headache. I certainly did.

15

If his dad and stepmother were angry when Nicky got home that night, he never told me about it. In fact, for the next week and a half he went through all the motions of normalcy without another word about the problem or his plans. I tried to tell myself his not talking about it was a good sign, but somehow it struck me as more ominous than anything he might have said.

Where could I go for help? Can you get help for something that hasn't happened yet? I spent a lot of time propped up in bed, Dandy scrunched in beside me, studying Daddy's photograph. I could have talked to him, Nicky could have talked to him, *everybody* could have talked to him!

Nicky was definitely a better actor than I was. Just about everybody close to me soon figured out something was wrong, except Mom, who was simply too busy to notice.

Mr. Hutton picked up on it the very next time I sat working at Mrs. Till's desk during study hall. Well, I wasn't exactly working. What I was doing was facing the typewriter, my fingers resting on the keys and my mind a million miles away, searching the galaxies for a solution.

"Hey, Connelly," Mr. Hutton called, charging into the office as if breaking through the line for a touchdown. "How's it going, sunshine?"

I snapped to attention. "Oh, okay, I guess," I said. A brief look around the desk reminded me that I was supposed to be addressing envelopes. I'd done four in thirty-six minutes. I whipped another envelope into the typewriter and started pounding away.

Mr. Hutton sat on the edge of the desk and gave me a long, hard look. "Nothing bothering you?" he asked.

"Uh-uh," I assured him, smiling as convincingly as possible.

"Your mom okay?"

"Uh-huh."

A kind of mist clouded Mr. Hutton's cool gray eyes, the very same eyes that flashed murder and mayhem when some troublemaker tried to cross him. "You miss your dad a lot, huh?" he asked softly.

I nodded. Nothing fake about that. I missed him, all right, more than ever, even if I didn't cry about it much anymore.

"These things take time," Mr. Hutton went on, beaming encouragement at me. It was hard to believe, just then, that some kids really hated his guts. He has such a nice craggy face, I thought, not handsome, but comfortable, like an old robe that folds around you just right on a winter day. I was sorely tempted to tell him about Nicky and ask him to do something before it was too late. The words were beginning to form on my tongue when he dropped a huge warm paw on my shoulder, then stood up, stretched and yawned noisily, and started out the door.

"Time to strike terror into the hearts of the wayward," he called back over his shoulder. "Carry on, Connelly."

Terror. If there was anything Nicky didn't need, it was terror. I couldn't report him and get him in trouble, not even if it meant losing him. Besides, he hadn't actually done anything yet, and maybe he never would. Why put him on Mr. Hutton's mental list of those requiring periodic doses of terror?

I attacked the envelopes before. me with renewed vigor. For a couple of minutes my fingers flew over the keys. Then I started thinking again—or at least trying to.

An avalanche of final exams and last-minute papers due came between Cara and my personal problems for a while, but she caught up with them at the hairdresser's the day before Spring Fling. So did Liz, who was there for what she called her "weekly overhaul." The three of us were flipping through magazines in the rustic waiting area when Liz casually asked me what Nicky and I had planned for the summer. I guess the expression on my face gave me away immediately.

"Uh-oh," she said, "nothing X-rated, I hope?"

I smiled at the irony of it and put down my magazine. "No. Nothing like that," I assured her. "Nicky's thinking of . . . well, of leaving town . . . for a while."

Cara shot me a surprised look. "You never mentioned that to me," she said.

"I'm mentioning it now," I replied. It was a weak attempt at lightheartedness. Cara and her mom ignored it.

"Leaving town for where?" Liz wanted to know.

"How long's a while?" Cara wondered.

"Anywhere," I said, lowering my eyes as they started

to puddle up with tears. I was so tired of trying to deal with the problem alone and getting nowhere. "Maybe Kansas City. Maybe forever."

Liz and Cara had been sitting diagonally across from me in the little three-sided square of padded wooden benches. Suddenly I had one of them on either side, and we were talking in hushed voices. Not that we needed to whisper. No one else was in the waiting area, a ceiling fan was whomping aerosol fumes at full speed over our heads, KCAT was bringing us the top forty over loudspeakers, and half a dozen blow dryers whined and whirred on the other side of the wooden fence that separated us from the operators' stalls. Still, we whispered, as if the topic were liable to explode.

"He's running away from home?" Liz said. "Is that what you're telling us?"

I nodded and filled in the details as well as I knew them.

"Wow," Cara breathed. "Does anyone else know about this? Does your mom?"

"No. I can't bear to tell her. Besides, why say anything beforehand? Maybe it'll never happen."

"But maybe it will," Cara pointed out. "What are you going to do?"

"What *can* I do? I tried to talk some sense into him, but he didn't want to listen. And lately he just avoids the whole issue."

"He seems okay to me," Cara mused. "On the other hand, maybe he seems *too* okay. Come to think of it, he jokes around a lot more than he used to, like he never lets the conversation turn serious. I've noticed that."

"Me too," I agreed. "And I don't like it."

Cara turned toward her mother, who seemed to be

studying the spinning fan above us. I followed her gaze involuntarily. The fan did have an alarming wobble.

"Mom," Cara said, "don't just sit there. *Say* something. *Do* something."

Liz slowly shifted her attention from the fan to us.

"Like what?" she asked. "If that's what he wants, he'll do it, with Heather's approval or without it. At least she's not making the mistake of taking off into the wild blue with him."

"He asked me to," I admitted.

"I'm not surprised," Liz said.

"But, Mom, it's so foolish," Cara insisted.

"Maybe. But we don't really know what goes on in other people's houses, do we? We don't know what pressures he's under. Besides, even if it is foolish, some people can't learn from other people's mistakes. They insist on making their own. God knows I'm living proof of that. Of course, there are those who still don't learn anything. Let's hope Nicky's one of the ones who do."

Nicky seemed high as a kite at the Spring Fling. For the first time ever, when someone else asked me to dance, he went off and found himself another partner, too. Once he and a junior girl got into such a contest of athletic prowess, everyone formed a circle around them and cheered them on till the music stopped. And *that* from a guy who once fled a Homecoming Dance in panic! If I didn't know better, I'd swear he was on something potent. But I did know better. In a few days the school year would end. He was high on the promise of freedom.

The semester ended on a Wednesday, the second day of an early-summer heat wave that was to go on for over two weeks before rain brought relief. The sun seemed to be pressing everything flat: buildings, trees, people, pigeons. Even poor Dandy was lifeless and took to spending most of the day beneath the hedge on the north side of our house.

At our old unairconditioned school there was no way to escape the heat. It seemed to throb against the drawn window shades in Mr. Hutton's office, where I'd stayed late to help straighten up the year-end mess. I hadn't wanted to stay, but Mrs. Till was swamped with last-minute details and I couldn't think of a good excuse not to. "Because my boyfriend may be running away today" sounded amazingly silly, for all its honesty.

Occasionally patting his face with a crumpled white handkerchief, Mr. Hutton whipped through his file cabinets, handing me papers and manila folders to run out to Mrs. Till's desk or stuff into one of three wastepaper baskets lined up between us. When the baskets were full, we lugged them to the bins in the basement, emptied them, then started all over again.

"Oh, if these old cabinets could talk," Mr. Hutton said, reading a handwritten memo before crushing it in his huge fist and tossing it my way. "Amazing how few people get through this place without getting some little note into their files they'd rather no one ever read. I suspect the ones who seem perfectly innocent just never got caught."

"Hmmmmm," I mumbled, dropping the wad of paper so I could hide my blush retrieving it.

"I like to send my seniors into the world with a clean slate," Mr. Hutton went on, already frowning into the next file folder. "What are your plans for the summer, Connelly?"

"Nothing special," I said. "I'm hoping to find a job.

I've filled out some applications, but haven't heard anything yet."

"Times are tough. What's the boyfriend going to do?"

My mouth fell open. "How did you know?" I gasped. Nicky and I were hardly the parade-down-the-hall-holding-hands-and-kiss-good-bye-before-every-class type.

Mr. Hutton grinned. "Ah, Connelly," he said, "an old pro like me can spot romance a mile away. Thank God my girls are all under twelve. I'm not ready for the drama, trauma, and broken hearts that lie ahead."

"How many girls do you have, Mr. Hutton?" I asked, interested but also eager to steer the conversation away from Nicky's summer plans.

"Three. Plus my wife and mother-in-law. I am a man adrift in a sea of women. Not that I'm complaining. I have managed to use my own bathroom twice in the last three years."

While I chuckled at that, he stomped one of his giant feet into a full basket, squishing the bulk of its contents to half. Maybe I could talk to him about Nicky without actually mentioning Nicky's name, I thought. Just call him "a friend," maybe. Mr. Hutton was certainly far from a terror-striking mood at the moment. In fact, he was probably feeling kind of fatherly, talking about his own daughters and all. I wondered if they could come to him with all their problems, and if he was always coincidentally in the mood for serious, silly, or just plain dumb.

Suddenly he slammed shut the bottom file drawer, scattering my thoughts. "Well, Connelly, I thank you for your assistance," he said. Draping a heavy arm around my shoulders, he walked me to the outer office door. "Next time I see you, you'll be a junior," he went on, looking kind of sad. "Funny how you kids keep aging and I don't." Then he gave me a gentle shove into the hall. "Take care, sunshine," he said.

A lump rose in my throat. Ever since Daddy's death, saying good-bye to my favorite people, even for a little while, really gets to me.

"You, too, Mr. Hutton," I managed to reply.

Alone in the shadowy hall, I fought with myself all the way to my locker. Should I have told Mr. Hutton about Nicky? Maybe. Probably? Or maybe not. Nicky had promised to call me before he took off—*if* he took off. Maybe now that the time was really here, he'd lose his nerve. I was all ready with my speech about how it didn't take guts to run away, it took guts to stay and work things out.

Anxious to get home, I spun my lock with shaking hands and yanked open the door. A piece of notebook paper fluttered off the shelf and landed, letter side up, at my feet.

16

Dear Heather,

I know I promised to talk to you before I did anything rash, but what's the point of doing something rash if you're going to pretty it up by keeping promises?

That was supposed to be funny, but if I know you, you're not laughing. Sorry. This is serious.

I feel bad about hurting you this way. I knew what you'd say, though, if we talked this over again, and I knew what I'd say. We'd just get into a fight. And I had to get away while Eve and Dad were still at work and the kids were with their sitter.

I'll be all right. I'll get in touch when I'm settled. I miss you already. I love you.

Nicky

I flew back upstairs toward Mr. Hutton's office, the rows of lockers and steps blurring on the far side of my tears. But when I got to the first-floor landing, Mr. Hutton was talking to a woman in the hall outside his office.

She was wearing slacks and a T-shirt and was handing him a baby wearing only a diaper.

I backtracked quickly before they could see me, then ran blindly through the tunnel, past the gym locker rooms, and out the basement door, where a wall of heat hit me, forcing me to stop and fight for breath. School is officially over, I told myself. He's just somebody's husband now, somebody's father. Somebody *else's* father, not yours.

Mom was still out when I got home. There were two phone calls that *should* have been Nicky, but weren't. The first was Mom saying she'd be a little late. The second was Mr. Simpson. He'd received a note from Nicky at his office. Apparently it said little more than mine.

"All I know for sure," I told him, "is that Nicky talked about going back to Kansas City."

"He didn't say who he was going to see?"

"He didn't mention any names," I said cautiously. Mr. Simpson sounded more puzzled than angry at the moment, but that didn't mean he was on Nicky's side.

"Did he tell you when he'd be in touch?" he asked.

"No. When he gets settled. Soon, I hope."

"Soon. How long is soon, I wonder?"

It was something we'd both have to wait to find out.

The sun had dried my tears, but a reserve supply seemed to have solidified in my chest. The weight lodged there for days, making sure Nicky was my last thought every night before I fell asleep and my first thought every morning as I awoke. In my dreams now, I ran down endless corridors, checking in room after room, calling his name. Sometimes I found Daddy, waiting behind a closed door, smiling, as if expecting me. But Nicky? Never.

With school out, I was more aware than ever of how little time Mom and I spent together. She'd added an aerobic dance class and a short course in car maintenance to her already hectic schedule. What time we did have was filled mainly with gossip about who dropped a wrench on whose toes and who treated herself to a hot fudge sundae the minute dance class was dismissed.

We did manage to watch a TV movie together that first Saturday night of vacation, curled up on opposite ends of the sofa with Dandy sprawled out between us.

"What's Nicky up to these days?" Mom asked during a commercial break. The question was bound to come, but it still caught me off guard. I'd been twirling a bit of Dandy's fur around my finger and he yipped as I gave it an accidental tug.

"Keeping busy," I managed to reply.

Mom raised her arms over her head and paused for a long, luxurious yawn. "I've never cared for Chinese food," she mused. "Too bad, or we could go to his restaurant some night and surprise him." She smiled my way, weariness lining her face.

The weight in my chest threatened to crack a rib, but I kept it to myself. For all her newfound interests and energy, she looked worn out. She was still losing weight, too. She needed Nicky inspiring her to bigger and better homemade pies, not burdening her with worry.

"Good movie," she murmured, shifting a pillow to support her head. "I love Mel Brooks." But before the film was half over, she'd fallen fast asleep.

Monday morning Mr. Simpson phoned me from work again and asked all the same questions, more insistently this time. It was hard to reconcile the smiling, nodding man I'd met with the harsh voice barking at me now. The long weekend of waiting had done him no good.

"You're sure he didn't tell you *anything* about who he went to see or *why*?" he asked.

I paused, considering my answer carefully. "Mr. Simpson," I said, "he did tell me why, but I don't think it's my place to tell you. I think Nicky has to do that. It's between Nicky and you."

"*What's* between Nicky and me? I have no idea of what you mean. Young lady, if you're keeping something from me, something I need to know about my son, I'd appreciate your speaking up. Or I could get in touch with your mother and insist—"

"No! Please don't bring my mother into this," I pleaded. "It's got nothing to do with her. I'll tell you everything I know. And I'll call you right away if I hear from Nicky. But please don't involve my mother. She really likes Nicky a lot, and I . . . I haven't told her about this. I keep thinking he'll come right back, so there's no point in upsetting her. My brother, my father, and my uncle are all gone, and she doesn't—"

"All right, all right," Mr. Simpson broke in, his tone softening. "I didn't mean to threaten you. I'm sorry. But if there is something you could tell me to help me understand, some hint of an explanation, I really would appreciate it."

As his voice faded into anxious silence, my sympathy for him grew. Forgive me, Nicky, I thought. This is probably not what you'd want me to do, but you're there —wherever "there" is—and your dad and I are stuck here.

"I know he's angry," I said, "at you and Mrs. Simpson and even the children."

"Angry?" Mr. Simpson exclaimed, a note of wonder in

his voice. "How is that possible? I honestly can't remember the last time I saw Nicky angry."

"Mr. Simpson, the way Nicky tells it, you and he
argue all the time."

"But we don't! I swear, we don't," he insisted, his
voice growing husky with emotion.

I believed him. And I believed Nicky, too. It was
crazy.

"Angry," Mr. Simpson repeated, as if trying to wring
an explanation from the word itself.

"Yes, angry," I said, "so he went to Kansas City to find
his mother."

For a moment I thought the line had gone dead—or
that Mr. Simpson had stopped breathing.

"He told you about her?" he said at last. "He hasn't
mentioned her in years. I thought he'd forgotten."

"He hasn't."

"My God," I heard him murmur, more to himself than
to me. Then, as if suddenly remembering I was still
there, he raised his voice and spoke quickly. "I—ah—I
have a lot to think about—ah—Heather. You will call if
you hear from him?"

"I will. I promise."

"Thank you. I mean that. You've been very helpful."
He gave me his number at the plant and hung up.

Helpful to you, maybe, I thought, still holding the
lifeless receiver, but I feel worse than before. I'd
thought I understood what Nicky was doing, even if I
didn't like it, but now I didn't even have that comfort.

"Why would Nicky lie to me?" I asked Cara later in
the day, after telling her about the phone call.

"Maybe he just told you his side," she said. "The
other side always looks different."

"That's true," I had to admit, "but how can you argue with someone and they don't even know you're angry?"

We were lounging at the neighborhood pool after another morning of filling out job applications and listening to variations on the theme of unemployment: "It's the economy." "Things are bad everywhere." "We're cutting back." "Try us next year."

"Only Nicky can figure that one out," Cara said, checking her shoulders for sunburn. "Stay tuned."

"How long?" I asked, fighting back a sudden surge of tears. "And what if he never—"

Cara patted my hand. "Be brave," she advised. "He'll be back."

I was being as brave as I knew how. As brave and as miserable.

"The hell with job-hunting," Cara announced, suddenly leaping to her feet and dragging me toward the pool's edge. "Tomorrow, let's go window-shopping at the mall. At least it's *air-conditioned.*"

With that, she belly flopped into the water, taking me with her.

17

"Wouldn't you know it?" I commented the next morning as Cara and I approached our favorite shoe store. "Just when we'd stopped looking."

There in the window was a SALESMAN WANTED sign.

"After you," Cara said. "You saw it first."

"It was your idea to come to the mall," I pointed out.

We hesitated, read each other's minds, then sailed through the doorway together. A salesman materialized in front of us immediately.

"Can I help you?" he asked. He wore a blue summer suit, was fresh out of college, I guessed, and looked like the type to spend a lot of time smiling in singles bars.

"Hi," Cara said, answering his plastic smile with one even brighter. "We'd like to apply for the job."

"The one in the window," I put in. "I mean, the sign's in the window, not the job."

It didn't matter what I'd said. He was already moving in on Cara. Oh, well, I thought, there goes that job. If I didn't like Cara so much, I could really hate her.

In one smooth maneuver the salesman took Cara's

arm and steered her over to the counter, away from other salesmen and customers. I hesitated, uncertain as to whether I was supposed to follow them or stay put. I compromised by shuffling into place beside Cara, but not too close.

"Forget it," the salesman told Cara confidentially. "The job's down here on the main floor. The owner won't hire a woman. Women go upstairs in bargain shoes."

"He won't?" Cara gasped. "Why not?"

"*She* won't," the salesman responded. "Because down here we're on commission. The shoes are more expensive and harder to move. She figures men are more aggressive, more competitive, and more desperate for money. She also figures rich ladies are more likely to turn loose of same when there's a young, attractive salesman involved." He grinned coyly, then bent his head so close to Cara's, they nearly touched.

Cara pulled back. "Thanks for saving us a lot of time and trouble," she told him, unhooking her elbow from his hand and slowly backing away.

The salesman shrugged modestly. "No big deal," he said. "But the next time you're in the market for a pair of shoes, ask for me. The name's Ted."

"Ted," Cara repeated thoughtfully, as if taking pains to memorize the name. "Ted, the next time I'm in the market for a pair of shoes, I will go anywhere on the planet Earth to buy them except here. Got that, Ted?"

Ted jerked his head back in surprise and alarm.

"As long as my feet live, they will never again step inside this store," Cara went on. "Tell your owner that for me, will you, Ted?"

With that, she hooked her arm in mine and we made out exit, jobless but triumphant. Once outside the store, we laughed ourselves breathless.

"It's good to see you laughing again," Cara said, eventually pulling herself together. "Life goes on."

"Boy, doesn't it!" I agreed. "Your mother would have been proud of you in there. That was Liz Dale all over."

The smile vanished abruptly from Cara's face, and her whole body sagged. "I wish you hadn't said that," she said.

"Why? I meant it as a compliment."

"Oh, I know. And I used to want to be just like her, but lately it kind of scares me."

"But the two of you are so close. . . ."

"That's part of the problem. There's already one Liz Dale. Who needs two? The more I think about it, the crazier it gets. To grow up, I have to become *more* like her, but to be *me*, I have to become *less* like her. How do I do that? How does anybody do that?"

"They just do, I guess."

"Or they don't," Cara shot back glumly.

"Oh, Cara, you have so much going for you," I insisted. "Come on, cheer up. Look, sixty million guys can't be wrong."

"Oh, yes, they can. What boys like about me isn't me at all. It's my brilliant imitation of *her*."

"That's not true!"

"True or not, that's how it feels to me. I tell you, Heather, I love her and I know she loves me, but two people can get *too* close."

That didn't seem possible to me.

Eddie called to say hi that evening. Mom was rushing out the door to yet another meeting just as the phone rang.

"Here, talk to your brother," she said, passing me the receiver. "Tell him I love him. I'll be home by eleven. Bye."

"Was that my mother?" Eddie asked. His voice seemed to be coming from the bottom of a well. "Doesn't she want to hear about my allergies? Do you know it never stops raining here? My sinuses must look like a swamp. Doesn't my own mother care?"

"Sure," I said, "but she's very busy these days."

"Good for her!"

"Guess so," I said, wishing I could share his enthusiasm.

"What's the matter, Heather? You don't sound so great."

"Oh, I'm okay."

"For some reason, I don't believe you."

"You don't want to hear about it, Eddie. You've got problems of your own."

"Nothing a good nasal spray wouldn't cure, but I'm allergic to them, too. Tell me."

"My boyfriend ran away."

"From you?"

"No," I said, giggling. "From his stepmother."

"Wait a minute. Haven't I heard this story before? She's wicked, right? And she dies in the end. He stuffs her in an oven. No, that's not it. He shoots her with a silver bullet."

I laughed till the tears came. Then the laughter stopped, but the tears kept right on coming.

"Oh, Eddie, I miss him so much. What am I going to do?"

"There's nothing much you can do, babe. Sounds like it's their problem. They'll have to solve it."

"I *hate* problems I can't solve!" I cried.

"I know. But you'll just have to wait this one out. Speaking of such, anything new with Uncle Will?"

"No."

"I got to thinking about him today. Remember when he—" Eddie's voice broke off in midsentence.

"Yes, I do," I said. "I remember every minute we ever spent with him."

"Yeah, me too. Listen, Heather, call me anytime you need to talk, okay? Call me collect. You'll get through this thing with Nicky. You're one tough kid."

"Thanks, Eddie," I said, grinning and snuffling back my tears.

"Anytime. Call me, okay?"

"Okay. Love to Marie."

"And hers to you."

As it turned out, I didn't call, but it was sure nice to know I could.

More than a week after he left, Nicky finally called.

"Where are you?" I asked. "Are you all right?"

"I'm in Kansas City. At a friend's house. I'm okay. How about you?"

"Pretty good, I guess, considering. Have you found a job? There's nothing here, absolutely nothing. People are even mowing their own lawns, or just letting them burn up in this heat."

"Not much better up here. I was offered this one job washing dishes in a greasy hole-in-the-wall. I'm sure the only reason the Department of Health hasn't closed it down is because they can't find it. There was no air conditioning in the kitchen and this one guy back there was sweating like a horse. The whole room stank. The guy whose job I'd be getting had just died. They didn't exactly say so, but I think he died right there in that kitchen."

"Good Lord, you didn't take the job, did you?"

"No, but if I get desperate enough, I may go back. I have a feeling it'll still be there."

"You could put that place in your book. How's it going? Are you getting lots of writing done?"

"Uh—no, not really. I'm out job-hunting most of the time. But I will, as soon as the dust settles."

"Good. Have you called your father and Eve?"

"No," he said, irritation snapping in his voice. "I'll call them when I'm ready, not before."

"Well—what about your mother? Any luck?"

"No. Not yet. Listen, I've got to go. I've got this egg timer and it's three minutes. I can't afford more. I'll try to call next week. I love you. Bye."

"Nicky, wait! Let me have your phone number. . . ."

But the line had already gone dead. I took a deep breath, lifted the receiver again, and dutifully dialed the number Mr. Simpson had given me. I felt like a spider, with a delicate web of phone lines spread out all around me. Only I couldn't use them to draw anyone closer. I could only sit perfectly still and hope the web wouldn't break.

18

Over the next few days, to pass the crawling minutes and empty hours, I renewed my efforts to train Dandy. We worked in the yard every morning after breakfast and in the evenings after the sun went down. It was an uphill battle, but one morning we finally achieved a major breakthrough: He agreed to come on command. Once, twice, three times in a row I let him wander away from me the length of the clothesline attached to his collar. And every time he came back when I called without my giving him the slightest tug. The third time I whirled him up into my arms and waltzed him into the house.

"Wait'll we show Nicky!" I cried. The empty house slapped back my words.

I put Dandy down, took a biscuit out of the canister on the kitchen counter, and tossed it into the air. Four paws off the ground, Dandy caught it on the fly. "Eddie Jr.," I mused, remembering how he'd come into our lives. "Now you're Nicky Jr., too. And Daddy Jr. And even Mom Jr. I don't know, Dandy, you're a great dog, but I don't think you can do it all alone. And neither can I."

I clenched my teeth against the sob rising in my throat. I've tried, I thought. I really have. I've stayed busy and cheerful and brave and everything else I can think of, but it's just not enough.

I waited for the crying jag to subside, then, still sniffling, I reached for the phone. The hospital switchboard made a couple of wrong connections before locating Mom. I had no plan, and yet the call seemed urgent.

"Heather? What is it? Is something wrong?"

"No," I said. "Well, yes. Well . . . I don't know. I was just sitting around the house with nothing to do and I wondered if maybe you needed some help over there."

"Oh? Why, no, not really. I don't think you'd enjoy it anyway."

"Try me," I said, surprising us both with my eagerness. "Maybe I will. You never know."

"Well, I do have to run a route myself today," Mom said. "Everyone's on vacation at once, it seems. It would go faster with two. . . ."

"Great! When should I come?"

"You sure you want to?"

"Yes. I really do."

"Okay. Be here by ten thirty. It's the north entrance, first door on your left."

I tossed Dandy one more biscuit and rushed upstairs to change from shorts to a sundress. I'd never been terribly interested in Mom's volunteer work. I still wasn't, but I *was* interested in Mom.

It was strange seeing her in an office, looking very much in charge of things with her glasses low on her nose, pen in hand and official-looking forms covering the top of her desk. It made me feel proud of her—and a little shy.

"Right on time," she said, straightening her glasses as she rose. "Let's go."

Taking her pen and a clipboard with forms on it, she led the way through a crowd of volunteers in the hall to a storage room filled with large Styrofoam coolers and a smell like stale, sticky pineapple. We each took a cooler and joined the group, which had begun moving down the hall. Everyone we met greeted Mom with a smile, a wave, or hospital in-jokes I didn't understand. She responded in kind, obviously pleased and comfortable with the attention. This was a side of her I'd never seen before: Mom in the Outside World—where she lived quite happily without me.

Around a corner we went, down a flight of concrete stairs and into the hospital kitchen. Along one wall were long stainless-steel tables loaded down with labeled brown lunch bags and rows of Styrofoam containers like covered TV-dinner trays. Along with the other volunteers, Mom and I located the section of meals for our route and began filling our coolers, checking off names against the list on her clipboard.

That done, our little army marched two by two out a loading-dock exit to the parking lot, where we shoved the heavy coolers into the backseats of our cars and set out to our assigned sections of the city.

I drove, Mom read the addresses from her list and gave directions. The first stop was at the crest of a hill almost at the city limits. The house stood last in a line of dilapidated shacks with peeling paint and weed-choked yards. I pulled into the gravel driveway and Mom hopped out, taking a lunch with her.

"You stay here," she said. "I'll be right back."

"Can't I come?" I asked.

She hesitated. "I suppose," she said slowly. "If you really want to. But you don't have to."

"I want to."

We picked our way carefully over the crumbling cement leading to the front door. A scrawny gray kitten scolded us, then disappeared into the weeds. Just as we reached the door, it opened, releasing a stench of urine that took my breath away. A tiny, ancient woman smiled up at us, but did not invite us in. She wore a clean white apron over a plaid dress, and her white hair was pulled back neatly into a bun, a striking contrast to the filth and odor that filled what I could see of her home. Newspapers were strewn everywhere, many of them wet. Two cats leaped off the tattered sofa behind her and a third slinked around her ankles and dashed outside. I fought the urge to turn and run and tried breathing through my mouth.

Mom stood her ground and greeted the woman like an old and dear friend.

"Hello, Mrs. Riknor," she said brightly. "It's so nice to see you again. Been a couple of weeks, hasn't it? Here's your lunch."

The woman took what was offered and continued to smile, but said nothing. Mom pulled the pen out of her pocket and began to read from her clipboard. "What would you like tomorrow?" she asked. "Hamburger or chicken?"

"Chicken," the woman whispered hoarsely.

Mom marked the list and continued reading off choices of vegetables, breads, beverages, and desserts. The woman responded mechanically.

"That's it for today," Mom told her at last. "Thank you, Mrs. Riknor, and I hope you enjoy your meal."

The woman said nothing, the door closed, and I stumbled on my way back down the path.

"Are they all like that?" I gasped when we were safely back in the car.

Mom shook her head. "The only thing they *all* are," she said, "is lonely."

There were five more names on our list. Mom got the next lunch out of one of the coolers as I drove on. This time we pulled up to a neat cottage painted yellow and bordered with beds of petunias. Mom rang the bell and we waited, baking slowly as the sun climbed the cloudless sky. She rang again. I glanced her way anxiously, wondering if we'd discover this one stone-cold dead, covered with newspapers and cats. What would we do? Mom, idly running a finger down her list, seemed unconcerned.

At last a faint voice instructed us to come on in. The door swung open at my touch. Inside, the shades were drawn, leaving everything in cool darkness. As Mom and I stood there squinting, our eyes struggling to readjust after the bright sun, a shadowy figure appeared from the hall and flipped on the overhead light. Our host was a tall, slender man wearing a painter's white jumpsuit. The room was neat as a pin. One black cat lay on a hassock, grooming herself daintily.

"Sorry to keep you waiting," the man said, blue eyes brilliant against the sunburned flush of his face and wispy white hair. "I've been out in the garden. Here, let me take that from you. I so appreciate you ladies bringing these lunches every day. It's hard for an old widower like me to remember to eat sometimes, you know that? I get caught up in my chores and I completely lose track of the time. Doctor says I must eat regular meals, though, so you ladies are really taking good care of me. Terribly hot outside, isn't it?"

On and on he went, about the weather, his garden, his age, and his health, while Mom listened and responded and deftly worked in her questions about the next day's menu, then maneuvered us back to our car through a quick tour of the garden. He stood beside the driveway and waved until we were out of sight, and Mom waved back.

A visiting nurse was on duty at our next stop; her patient was too ill to see us. The nurse ordered the next day's meal briskly, and we were soon on our way again.

The two clients after that were men, one elderly and confined to a wheelchair, the other up and about and seemingly too young and healthy to be in need of Home Meals. The first man wept as he told us his daughter had just left for Arizona after a two-week visit. "She comes twice a year," he explained between apologies for his tears. "I'm fine most of the time, really I am. It's just after she leaves, though . . ."

Mom sat by his side and listened for quite some time. I stood in the shadows fighting back tears of sympathy and more than a little self-pity. My admiration for Mom was growing at the same rate as my own feelings of uselessness. I had no place in this part of her life. Did I have a place in *any* part of her life at all? Or anybody else's life, for that matter?

Three blocks away, the younger man scolded us for being late and complained about the food, the next day's choices, the welfare system, and several governmental agencies I'd never heard of. Mom listened patiently to all of that, too. I didn't think he deserved the kindness she showed him, but she showed it just the same.

The woman at our last house was very old and bent almost double by the hump deforming her back. She sat in an armchair, propped up by an assortment of colorful pillows, and waved us in through her screen door.

"On a good day, I'd get up and let you in myself," she said, laughing, "but this isn't a good day, I'm afraid. Weather must be about to change."

"Rain, do you think, Mrs. Moberly?" Mom asked, offering her the lunch tray and sack.

"I certainly hope so," Mrs. Moberly answered. "Please put that on the kitchen table. I'll get to it by and by."

Mom took a moment to introduce me as her daughter, something she'd been doing all morning, but Mrs. Moberly was the first person to show much interest in making my acquaintance.

"Always wanted a daughter," she said, with an affectionate pat on my arm. "My sons are fine boys, but I don't care what anybody says, girls are different. My mama and me—why, she's been gone thirty-four years, but it does me good to this day to think about the times we had."

As Mom left the room, Mrs. Moberly inclined her head toward me confidentially. "Actually," she said, "I always figured God made Adam for practice. Then, when He got the kinks out, He made Eve. Told my Sunday-school teacher that in fourth grade," she continued with a snicker. "Got sent straight to the preacher. My daddy was mad, but my mama, she laughed and laughed."

Somehow it wasn't hard to picture that gnarled old woman as a mischievous child. Mom returned to find the two of us laughing, and smiled in surprise. Laughter did seem like a foreign language that morning. As Mom sat on a stool facing Mrs. Moberly, the old woman immediately began reading the chart on her lap upside down.

"Hamburger!" she cried. "I don't suppose they mean McDonald's. My neighbor brings me two or three of those a week. I just can't get enough of those fries. In this case, though, I better put my money on the chicken."

Mom and I left the house still chuckling.

"I'm going to miss her," I admitted. "I just met her and I'm going to miss her. Isn't that amazing?"

Mom nodded, her shoulders suddenly drooping. Even with my help, the trip had taken nearly two hours, and the heat was worse than ever. She slipped a tissue out of her purse and dabbed at the beads of perspiration above her lip.

"Don't get too attached," she said. "The regular drivers will be back next week."

"How do you keep from getting attached?" I wondered, holding the car door while Mom settled herself inside.

"I don't know," she said softly. "But it's something you have to do."

I slid into the driver's seat and watched as she removed her glasses and rubbed her eyes. The good cheer she'd shown everyone on our route was visibly draining away.

"You look pooped," I told her. "Don't you think you ought to come home?"

"No, no. I'm fine. Besides, I have to see that everyone's checked in and then I thought I'd stop by and see Uncle Will. I haven't been there in over a week."

"How often do you go?"

"Twice a week, usually. Wednesdays and Saturdays."

"Why haven't you ever told me?"

"What's the point? He doesn't know who's there and who isn't. I just like to make sure he's getting proper care."

"But I'd like to go. I'll go now. You don't have to do it all."

"Oh, Heather, haven't you seen enough misery for one day?"

I had. More than enough. But I was desperate to do

something for her, to fit myself somewhere into this world that seemed to be spinning away from me faster and faster. And she *was* tired. She could no longer hide it, but for some unfathomable reason, she refused to admit it.

"Mom, he's my *uncle*," I insisted. "If I can visit all these strangers, shouldn't I spend some time with my own uncle? I want to go. I really do. And it'll save you a trip."

"All right," she conceded. "But stop by my office for a minute. I have a couple of things you need to take with you."

With a last look at Mrs. Moberly's little white house, I started the car and headed back to the hospital. What Mom had for Uncle Will was a bouquet of black-eyed Susans from Daddy's garden and a glass jar filled with jelly beans.

"Does he eat jelly beans?" I asked.

Mom managed a chuckle. "The flowers are for him," she explained. "Set the jelly beans on his night table. It's a good way to make sure the nurses and aides stop by often to check on him. He can't ask them to, and you never know. They get busy; they get careless."

"You think of everything, don't you?" I said.

She eased herself into the chair behind her desk. "I wish 'everything' were enough," she murmured.

It had, as Nicky once said, a familiar ring to it.

19

I had not seen Uncle Will since he'd been moved from the hospital to the nursing home, and I'd only seen him once in the hospital. A niece who bursts into tears at the foot of your bed is not exactly what the doctor ordered. I was determined to handle this visit more maturely.

As I pulled into the parking lot of the Green Valley Convalescent Home, I was remembering him as he used to be: a larger, heavier, louder, even funnier version of Daddy. His apartment in our basement was always open to Eddie and me, and he never turned down Eddie's dungeon-and-dragon challenges or a trip to the pool to watch me show off my awkward attempts at diving.

I could hardly remember Aunt Gayle, who'd died of leukemia. Because of her long illness she and Uncle Will never had children of their own. "Never had the good fortune" was the way Uncle Will always put it if anyone asked. Whenever Eddie and I got in trouble with Mom and Dad, we'd remind them that we were their "good fortune." It worked, now and then, to get us off easy.

The glass doors of the home opened onto a large visiting area. Tile walls, slick floors, air conditioning, and the smell of antiseptic overwhelmed my senses as I entered. It took a moment for the odor of decay to seep through and the figures scattered around the lobby to come into focus. Frail and bent, they sat quietly talking, reading, or just staring straight ahead. One man paced from one picture window to the next, as if waiting for someone to arrive in the parking lot. I soon realized, though, that his movements were mechanical and made no sense. If he was waiting, he'd probably forgotten for whom.

I asked for Uncle Will's room at the reception desk, then followed the receptionist's curt directions to the farthest of four hallways opening off the visiting area. Moans, mutters, soft weeping, and television voices reached out to me from the rooms I passed. A tight-lipped nurse hurried by, giving no sign at all that she'd noticed my presence.

At Room 103, I turned in. The first thing I saw was the window. The shade had been pulled all the way to the top and sunlight was streaming in, nearly blinding me with its intensity. I put the jelly beans and flowers on the floor and quickly lowered the shade partway. When I turned back, I saw Uncle Will. I sank into the chair beneath the window.

He was half the size I remembered him, and his fringe of hair had turned completely white. He could have been his own ghost—or Daddy's. His bed was raised so that he was sitting nearly erect, his hands resting awkwardly atop a light blanket, the nails long, thick, and yellowed. His eyes followed me without expression as I stood up and moved closer. Once a light, sky-bright blue, they now glinted like black beads. The pupils were so enlarged—in spite of the sunlight still bathing the room—there was hardly any rim of iris left. His dry, chapped lips parted slightly as I approached the side of his bed. I paused, waiting for him to say something, but he simply went on watching me quietly. Maybe he was expecting food or medication. Maybe there just wasn't anything to say.

"Oh, Uncle Will," I whispered. "Oh, Uncle Will, I am so sorry."

I sat on the edge of the bed and took Uncle Will's icy hand in mine. Try as I might to control them, tears began to pour down my face, tears for Uncle Will, for all the lonely people I'd seen that morning, for Daddy, for Nicky, for myself. "I love you, Uncle Will," I told him, rubbing the tears away with my free hand. "I hate seeing you like this, but I love you just the same. I wish there was something I could do. I'd do anything—"

"No point to it," a voice interrupted.

Startled, I dropped Uncle Will's hand and spun around. A fat woman in a white uniform had entered the room. Grunting as she stooped over, she picked up the flowers and the jelly beans. "He don't know what you're talking about," she said. "Where do you want these here?"

"The flowers can go on the windowsill, I guess, where he can see them. You're welcome to have some jelly beans."

"Thanks. Might as well. He'll never miss 'em."

"Are you a nurse?" I asked, hoping she was a cleaning lady or something like that, someone who had little to do with Uncle Will.

"Nurse's aide. Nurses don't spend much time with

him. Medication, stuff like that. I do the rest. Feed 'em, clean 'em up. Name's Milly. You his daughter?"

"No, I'm his niece. He has no children," I told her. "Never had the good fortune," I added softly.

I don't think she heard me, not that she was listening. She set the flowers on the table beside Uncle Will, where he'd have to turn his head to see them, then shook a hill of jelly beans into her well-padded hand. When she was satisfied she could hold no more, she put down the jar and popped three or four beans into her mouth.

"You know what that is?" she asked, nodding toward Uncle Will and munching her mouthful thoughtfully. "That's about as alone as you can get in this life." Mistaking my stunned silence for interest, she swallowed hard and went on. "My daughter took me over to the university to see Lily Tomlin not long ago. You ever seen Lily Tomlin?"

"On television. And in the movies."

"Right. Anyway, so there she was, doing all this funny stuff, and all of a sudden, she falls down flat on her back—right there in the middle of the stage. And she lies there for a minute and then she says something like, 'Notice how many come up here to see what was wrong?' Nobody, of course. 'Just remember,' she says, 'we are all in this alone.' "

Milly nodded toward Uncle Will again, all the while refilling her supply of jelly beans. "Thought of these people right then and there," she mused. "That's exactly what it is. All in this alone. 'Course, it comes to everybody sooner or later."

My heart began to pound as both rage and fear enveloped me.

"Uncle Will is not alone," I said. "He's got my mother. He's got me."

Brow furrowed, Milly concentrated on balancing her mound of candy in one hand as she replaced the jar on the night table. "Whatever you say, hon. Thanks for the snack," she said, then waddled out the door, one thick white stocking sagging around her ankle.

A shudder passed through me, then I turned back to Uncle Will. He'd slumped deeper into the pillow supporting him, his head lolling to one side, his eyes closed. I sat watching him until the emotions boiling inside of me quieted down.

"Some of us are in this *together*," I whispered, brushing a kiss across the stubble on his cheek without disturbing his sleep. "It's possible. It has got to be. But it sure isn't easy."

I tiptoed over to the flowers, placed them on the windowsill where they'd be the first thing he'd see when he woke up, and left.

Mom's car was still gone when I pulled into our driveway. Dreading the emptiness of our house, I brought Dandy out of the backyard and sat with him under the old hard maple tree on our front lawn. It was my old climbing tree; every summer I'd inch my way a few branches higher to spy on the neighborhood and daydream. Now I could see heat shimmering off everything beyond its leafy shade.

Some time later Cara and her mom got off the bus at the corner of our block and began walking toward their house. Similarly dressed in T-shirts, denim skirts, and sandals, they looked like sisters. Cara, being slightly larger and heavier, actually appeared to be the older of the two from that distance. I wondered what her father looked like. Immediately an image of K. A. McKuen, the Human Typhoon, sprang to mind. Definitely the type with whom you could make a mistake for want of things to talk about.

The sound of laughter drifted toward me, and I watched as Liz wrapped an arm around Cara's shoulder, drawing her closer as they shared a joke. An aching loneliness swept over me and I had to look away. Bowing my head, I stroked Dandy's soft fur as he lay at my feet, panting.

That Saturday night the heat wave finally broke. I was sound asleep when a clap of thunder brought me upright. Rain was blowing in my window and had already soaked the sill and part of my carpet. Mom and I staggered from room to room lowering sashes, stopping only to marvel sleepily at the downpour and the explosions of lightning zigzagging the sky.

It was quieter, but still raining hard, when I awoke again early Sunday morning. Barefooted and in my nightgown, I pulled on a raincoat and made a dash across the lawn toward the orange plastic bag containing our newspaper. I'd just plucked it out of the mud when I noticed a car parked on the south side of our driveway. I blinked away the rain to make sure, half expecting the car to evaporate before my eyes. But it didn't.

Leaping over puddles, ignoring the gravel digging into the soles of my feet, I raced down the driveway. It was Nicky's old Dodge Dart, all right. The windows were rolled up. Through the streaming rain I could see Nicky asleep on the backseat, scrunched up on his side like a child. I tried the doors, but they were locked. I banged on a window with my fist.

"Nicky? Nicky! Wake up!"

He raised himself on one elbow and shook his head groggily, then saw me, sprang awake, unlocked the door, and scrambled out. Never mind that I was wearing nothing but a nightgown and raincoat. Never mind that I was sopping wet, with hair soaked and plastered to my face. We hugged each other until our arms ached, then kissed and hugged each other some more.

"How long have you been out here?" I asked.

"Most of the night. Your house was dark, and anyway, I was afraid you'd be too mad to let me in."

"I am. I'm furious," I said, laughing. "But I'll let you in anyway. Come on, before we drown."

We could hardly let go of each other long enough to dry our faces and get the coffee started. I tiptoed upstairs to get my robe, dying to wake Mom up and share the good news with her. I paused for a moment outside her door as a chill of realization ran through me: She didn't even know it *was* good news. We knew almost nothing about each other, nothing important. We were living miles apart under the same roof, talking without saying anything, sharing only our meals.

Moving more slowly now, I gathered up my robe and a couple of towels and went back downstairs to Nicky.

"I guess you never found a job, huh?" I said after we'd rubbed our hair dry and shuffled our chairs right up against each other at the kitchen table. We were sitting so close, we could have made do with one cup of coffee.

"No. Even that awful dishwashing job was taken when I got back. Oh, Heather, the whole thing was such a mess, you'll never believe it."

"Tell me. I'll believe it. Tell me everything, from the beginning."

"It's all very stupid and embarrassing," Nicky protested.

"What a coincidence!" I said. "I've been in the mood for stupid and embarrassing all week."

Nicky laughed, as I knew he would, and began his story.

"I went straight to my aunt Kate's house. She's not really my aunt, but she and my mother were best friends, had been since they were kids, so I called her my aunt. She and my father never could stand each other; he's so straight and she's kind of wild. Anyway, after my mother left, she used to invite me over on the sly now and then, when my dad wasn't around, to make sure I was okay. She'd warn me not to tell him where I'd been, because he'd never let me come back."

"So that's why your father never thought to call her," I said. "He's been calling everyone else. He's been worried sick."

Nicky's face fell. "No. He called her. He finally figured it out, couple of nights ago. You still want the whole story, or should I skip to the end?"

"The whole story," I said.

"Yeah, well, there I was at Kate's front door. At first, she was thrilled to see me. Hugs, kisses, the whole bit, just the way I'd imagined it the whole time I was driving up there. Then she introduces me to her new husband—number three or maybe four. He gets out a few beers, everybody drinks a toast to my health, and then wham! You should've seen their faces when I said I needed to stay with them for a while. If I could've taken the words back, snatched them right out of the air and shoved them back down my throat, I would have. But it was too late. They didn't want to say yes, but they did. What choice did any of us have? I mean, there I was!

"I've never felt so alone in my life. Every day when they got home from work, first thing out of their mouths was: 'Did you find a job?' It got so I couldn't stand telling them I hadn't day after day, so I took to eating dinner at a hot dog stand and wandering the streets till I was so tired I could go straight to bed."

"Oh, Nicky, they sound like creeps."

"No, they're not. You have to see it their way. I mean, they'd only been married a couple of months and here they were stuck with a sixteen-year-old kid and no end in sight."

"I guess you didn't get any writing done, either."

A derisive snicker escaped Nicky's throat, then he pushed his chair away from the table and went to the counter to refill his cup. "I'm so full of crap," he said, his back still toward me.

"What do you mean?" I asked.

When he turned around, his face was drawn and tears glittered in his eyes. "I never wanted to be a writer," he said. "I've never even written a limerick."

"But you told me—"

"I know what I told you, and I believed it myself. But what I really wanted to be was a famous author, so my mother would see my name on the best-seller list and get in touch with me and tell me how terrific I was and how much she loved me and how sorry she was she'd left me. That's what I wanted."

He had just time to put down his cup before the sobs wrenched themselves up from his chest. I ran to his side, but he turned away toward the counter, so I wrapped my arms around him and pressed my cheek against his back.

"Oh, God, Heather," he said, shuddering, "what you must think of me now."

"I think you're sad, Nicky," I told him. "I think you have every right in the world to be sad. What she did to you, what she's doing to you, is rotten. It's terrible and hurtful and wrong."

"At first I thought Kate was lying to protect her. But she wasn't. She hasn't heard from her either, not once in all these years, and they were best friends. She's gone, Heather. I can hope and I can dream and I can pretend till the day I die—and I guess I will—but I can't change it. She's gone."

I took him by the shoulders and made him turn around. Ashamed of his tears, he tried looking everywhere except into my eyes, but eventually he had to face me.

"It's her loss, too," I told him. "She's really missing out. Believe me, I know. I love you, and I'm no fool."

Eyes still brimming with tears, Nicky grinned. "You sure about that?" he said.

"Positive." And I proved it with a long, rather salty kiss.

"Anyway," Nicky went on, "by the time Dad called and asked me to come home, I was ready."

"I'm glad. I mean, I'm sorry things didn't work out the way you'd hoped, but I'm glad you're back."

Nicky nodded, then broke into the thoughtful silence that followed. "I . . . um . . . I don't know exactly how to bring this up," he said, "but could I have something to eat? I'm starving."

"Of course!" I cried. "Scrambled eggs? Rice Krispies? Toasted bagels?"

"All three. Anything but a hot dog. All I had for dinner last night was a Coke. I'm out of money. Gas, food, the car broke down twice. Aunt Kate and number three or four didn't exactly fall all over themselves offering me a loan."

"Sit down. You'll find our rates very reasonable," I told him, and set about filling his order—doubling it, actually, as I suddenly found myself ravenously hungry, too. Outside, the rain had dwindled to a drizzle, but the sky still hung low and dark with clouds.

"What did your dad say when he called?" I asked as we dug into our feast.

"Come home. We miss you. We're worried about you. Stuff like that. Come home and we'll talk."

"Come home and we'll talk. That sounds good."

"I guess so. Of course, I told him I'd have to think about it, but the truth is, I miss them and I'm worried about them and I want to go back. I never thought I'd be saying that, but it's true."

"Oh, Nicky, that's wonderful. But what happened? Why the big change?"

"One thing I had plenty of in Kansas City was time to think. And every day I stayed away, things got a little muddier up there and a little clearer down here. I love my dad; I've always loved him. He could've pawned me off on somebody else when my mother left, but he didn't. I owe him for that. And Eve loves him, too. She really tries to make him happy, even though they're having a rough time at work. They don't know from one day to the next whether that plant's going to shut down or move to Japan or lay them off. They had to elope that weekend because the management disapproves of what they call 'employee involvement.' You're allowed to be married, but not to date."

"They told you that?"

"No. I was too busy sulking after they got home. Jeal-

ousy, pure and simple. Dad was all I had and I'd had
him all to myself. I heard them explaining the situation
to friends. Of course, I went right on sulking. I was
angry at them for getting married, for not telling me
and for dragging those two little brats into my house.
You know, they're a real pain in the neck sometimes,
but every morning I'd see these kids playing in a school-
yard up there and I'd miss those little brats, I really
did."

"Nicky," I interrupted, "you're going to hate me for
this, maybe, but I told your dad you were angry and he
couldn't believe it. He said you and he never fight."

"We don't."

"But all those times our plans got upset—"

"I argue with her, not him. The minute he walks in
the door, we pretend nothing is wrong."

"But why?" I asked, in amazement.

Nicky shrugged. "We both want to look like perfect
angels to *him,* I guess. But even if she'd moved in wearing a halo and wings, it wouldn't have mattered to me.
What a show I put on: I baby-sat, I cleaned house, I
shoveled snow. But only after the two of us had gone a
couple of rounds over it behind his back. Then, every
minute I did help out, I was wishing he'd say, 'Hey,
look at that Nicky. He's so great, what do I need the
rest of them for?' She knew it, too. I made sure of that.
What could she do? Tell her new husband his only son
was a creep?"

"Wow," I said. "And here I always thought you were
twins. Maybe you're triplets: one sweet, one sad, and
one *rotten.*"

"Yeah, yeah, I know. Well, it didn't do me any good
anyway. The more I did, the less he noticed. He was so

busy running around in circles at that plant, he turned me over to her like an extra set of car keys."

"But that's it, Nicky," I broke in. "Don't you see? He's busy and he's worried and he's gotten used to counting on you. He sees a nice, obedient, helpful guy with good grades, a job, his own car and a girlfriend, and he figures you're *set*. You've got everything you need." As I spoke, urgency rising in my voice, I became aware of something like a pinpoint of light flickering at the back of my mind.

"I need him, too," Nicky said. "Him *especially*. I wouldn't mind helping out, I really wouldn't. I just want . . . They've got each other now, and the kids. I feel like I'm hanging on the edge by my fingertips, about to fall off."

"Tell him. *Say* something. 'Come home and we'll talk.' He means that, so *do* it!"

I waited anxiously for Nicky's response. It was important to him, but every bit as important to me.

He looked at me for a long moment, then let out the breath he'd been holding. "You're right. That's what I've got to do," he said. "How'd you get so smart?"

"I'm not," I admitted, the flickering pinpoint of light growing wide and steady until it seemed to flood my brain. "Oh, Nicky, I've been making the exact same mistake. My mom says mothers are born with good hearing, but I've been wanting her to hear something I've never said out loud. You know, it's too bad we don't all have heartlights like E.T., little red glows we couldn't hide, so we'd know right away when somebody was in love or in need."

I was dead serious, but Nicky threw his head back and roared with laughter. "Great idea," he said, "I can just see the two of us in geometry, bathing the class in our bright crimson glow."

I began to giggle. "Wouldn't be any more embarrassing than what we went through trying to make contact the human way," I protested.

"Nicky! Haven't seen you in a while. Have you been sick? You've lost so much weight."

Nicky and I spun around to see Mom standing in the doorway in her robe, fingering her sleep-mussed hair and regarding Nicky with concern.

Nicky's mouth opened slightly as he rose from his chair about to answer, then opened even wider as it dawned on him that Mom knew nothing of his adventure. He sent an alarmed look my way. At the same time, Mom's eyes darted between us, concern quickly fading into confusion and suspicion.

"I've been to Kansas City," Nicky began.

"And now he's going home," I concluded quickly.

21

"You would have told your father."

Nicky was gone, Mom was sitting stiffly at the kitchen table, and I was pouring her a second cup of coffee with hands that were still shaking. I set the cup down hard in surprise.

"Probably," I admitted. "But everything might have worked out differently if Daddy were alive. He and Nicky might have talked it all over long ago."

"Why didn't you tell me?" she asked, very softly.

"Lots of reasons," I said. "I didn't want to upset you. I didn't want you to be disappointed in Nicky."

"There's a lot of Daddy in you," she observed. "You don't like to make trouble."

She'd mentioned him twice, I realized. Maybe something was moving, changing at last for us. Maybe the right time had finally come.

"Mom," I said, sitting beside her in the chair Nicky had used, "I want to talk about Daddy with you. I want to be able to remember him out loud with you."

"I don't understand," Mom said.

"This is the first time we've mentioned him in months,

do you realize that?" I asked. "I think about how much he would've enjoyed watching Dandy grow up, and how much he would've liked Nicky. I want to be able to say that out loud, and to reminisce about the crazy way he used to sing and how he'd slap himself on the head when we'd laugh at him. I want to say things like that to you all the time, but I can't. It always seems as if we'd have to cry first if I even said his name. Even about the happy things, we'd have to get past the tears first, and you don't seem to want that."

Mom sat watching me with an anxious, helpless expression, as if she wanted to say something but couldn't, and was hoping I'd say it for her.

"I've never seen you cry since he died," I went on. "I've never heard you speak his name until today. I've tried to push him out of my mind and just go on, the way you've done, but I can't. I don't understand how you've managed it. I've cried an ocean alone in my room, I mean it. The Bernard Connelly Memorial Sea."

Mom sat back in her chair and folded her hands in her lap. "So have I," she whispered.

"You have? But why are we doing it in secret? Is it something to be ashamed of?"

Mom studied her hands for a while, stroking one thumb against the nail of the other while I waited.

"I've tried to keep busy," she began hoarsely. "I've tried to stay out of your way because I knew if I opened up at all, even the slightest bit, I'd end up leaning on you the way I leaned on Daddy. I do not want to be a burden to you or to anyone else ever again. That's what I'm ashamed of, not the grief."

"But you've never been a burden," I said. "What are you talking about?"

"Your father did everything for me, everything he

could think of to please me. Ours wasn't a fifty-fifty marriage, it was about ninety-ten. After a ninety-ten day with his miserable partner, he'd come home to another ninety-ten day with me. We wore him out."

"Mom, that's crazy. Maybe Joe Brady wore him out, but not you. Daddy loved making you happy. The look on his face when you woke up and saw Dandy that first morning—it was priceless. He told me, Mom, he said that from the day he met you, he was the happiest person in the world."

"He said that?"

"He did, and he meant it. Besides, there were lots of things you did for him. And for Eddie and me and Uncle Will. You're always doing things for people, lots of little extra things you don't have to do, like fixing our favorite meals and putting flowers and candles on the table—and the bouquet and jelly beans I took to the nursing home."

"Little things, that's all I do," Mom insisted. "And even that, I learned from Daddy. In my family, it was a kiss on the cheek for your birthday and at weddings, and that was supposed to hold you as far as affection went. The night my father died, I got home just as the ambulance was pulling away. I ran into the house and found my mother, my aunts, and my uncle standing around the living room, each of them separate and frozen like actors who'd forgotten what to do next. Without thinking, I rushed up to my mother and threw my arms around her. She didn't budge, and when I stepped back, they were all staring at me as if I'd done something terribly inappropriate. I don't know why I did what I did. Hugging was for five-year-olds, and I was twenty-three. I don't know why it was so foreign to them, either, but that's the way it was."

I thought back to the day Daddy had died. Mr. Hutton had brought me home. Mom was red-eyed but calm as she met us at the door and thanked him. Then she'd gone into the kitchen to call Eddie and make all the necessary arrangements and I'd run up to my room to cry. That wasn't *right*.

I remembered Marie putting her arm around Mom's shoulders in the waiting room during Daddy's funeral. Mom had ignored her and stopped Eddie when he'd tried to speak. That wasn't right, either.

"They were good people, your grandparents," Mom went on. "I'm not saying they were mean or cruel. They just never had anyone like your father, I guess, to teach them how to love. I learned everything from him, Heather. I took and I took and I could never give enough back."

"You gave him everything he ever wanted, Mom."

She bowed her head, one small fist pressed against her trembling lips. "I don't know," she murmured. "Oh, Heather, we were so lucky to have him. And then, when he died, he was all alone."

"Oh, no," I cried, shoving aside my coffee cup and reaching for Mom's hand as the tears cascaded down both our faces. "He wasn't alone, not really. You mustn't think of it that way. Daddy wouldn't. He knew we loved him; he never doubted it for a minute."

We held hands and wept and noticed how the rain was gusting harder against the windowpanes again and laughed at the irony of it, then went on weeping.

"He left us each other, Mom," I said at last, getting up to supply us with tissues from the box on the counter. "It's bad enough when you lose someone to death, or when you can't reach out to anybody, like Uncle Will, or when you reach out and the other person refuses, like

Nicky and his mother. But you and I are in this together. We shouldn't let go of that. We should work on
it, hold on to it."

"I suppose so," Mom said, her words muffled by the
tissues. She wiped her eyes and nose, then sat quietly
watching the rain. "Still, I have to learn to stand on my
own two feet. You won't be with me forever. You already have your own friends, your own life. You'll be
going off to college soon, then you'll be gone for good,
like Eddie."

"Eddie's *away*, Mom, not gone. There's a big difference. If we needed him, he'd be here in no time. If he
needed us, we'd be on the first plane out. You know
that's true."

"Yes," Mom said, drawing the word out slowly, "but
whatever you say, I do not want to be a burden. I don't
want to saddle you with my endless needs."

"There's got to be a place in between," I insisted.
"Between a burden and a . . . a missing piece. I want
you in my life. I want to be part of yours."

"That's what I want, too," Mom said, eyes glittering.
"I always have. I just don't know how—"

"To make the puzzle fit. Me neither. But there's got to
be a way."

22

Thanksgiving, 1982, was also different. Uncle Will had gone to sleep one muggy August afternoon and never woke up again. Having attended his funeral, Eddie and Marie couldn't afford another trip in for the holiday. But Cara and Liz stayed in town.

"They're planning to eat at a restaurant," I told Mom. I was wheeling a cart down a grocery aisle as we shopped for the long weekend's supplies.

"Oh, we can't let them do that, can we?" Mom asked. "Maybe they'd like to eat with us?"

"Great idea. Why don't you give Liz a call when we get home?"

"Oh, well, you can do it. They're your friends."

"Mom, they're *our* friends. Yours and mine. We're all in this together, remember?"

I ended up making the call, but that's okay. At least it got made. At first Mom was set on preparing the entire meal herself, but Liz finally convinced her to let everyone share the load. So Cara and I took turns out back manning the turkey on Daddy's grill, and we all swarmed over the kitchen and dining room, preparing a banquet for an army of four. Dandy rushed indoors and out, doing his best to get in everyone's way at once.

After dinner Liz shooed Cara and me out of the kitchen. "Never mind the dishes," she said when I protested. "It's time your mother and I got reacquainted."

Nicky was due over soon from his family's dinner for a second dessert, so I didn't mind the chance to tidy up. Cara was unusually quiet as she tagged along from bathroom to bedroom and back downstairs, where she plopped down on the sofa and heaved a mighty sigh.

"So," she said, "how are things going at Nicky's house?"

"Pretty good," I said. "Eve had her whole family over for dinner today. Things are working out, slow but sure."

"You know, Heather, I believe you have finally scored a first on me."

I sat back on my heels in front of the bookcase, where I'd begun replacing cookbooks we'd consulted earlier in the day. "What do you mean?" I asked.

"You're always talking about how I do everything before you do, but you're the first to have a real boyfriend."

"Oh, come on, you've had sixty million—"

"Admirers, dates, fans, guys to have fun with as long as it didn't turn too serious. Cake without the calories. It never lasts long. No, you've done it, Heather. You've pulled ahead of me. You've weathered the ups and the downs, the for better and for worse. What you have here is *love*."

"I know," I said softly, a grin like a wave of warmth starting all the way down in my toes and quickly working its way up.

Cara yanked a throw pillow off the seat beside her

and hugged it to her chest. "Which brings me to the big question," she went on. "Is there something wrong with me? Is there something missing?"

Shaking my head emphatically, I stood up. Lamplight reflecting off the glass in a picture frame caught my eye. It was the photo of Daddy I'd brought down from my bedroom one rainy day last summer. What would he have told Cara? I wondered, then tried to listen to all the wise and loving words he'd left in my heart.

"You know what?" Cara said. "Sometimes I think I eat like a pig to fill up my empty places, to build more *me.*"

I turned around to face her, but she buried her face in the pillow's thick fringe. "You don't eat like a pig," I told her. "You're not fat, you're not a pig, and you're not a second-rate Liz Dale. You're you and you're fine. No. You're *terrific.* What's it going to take to convince you of that?"

Lifting her head, Cara revealed a shy, uncertain smile. "I don't know," she admitted. "But do me a favor? Keep trying?"

"Bank on it," I told her. And we daughters of accountants don't say those words lightly.

ABOUT THE AUTHOR

SANDY ASHER is the author of five novels for young people, as well as of plays, poems, stories, and articles that have appeared in numerous publications. In 1978 she received a playwriting grant from the National Endowment for the Arts. Teaching, gardening, cooking, dance class, and racquetball occupy much of her time when she is not writing. She lives in Springfield, Missouri, with her family and teaches creative writing at Drury College. Her most recent novels for Delacorte Press were *Just Like Jenny* and *Things Are Seldom What They Seem*.